The Cowboy's Christmas Retreat

—

CATHERINE MANN

D0210179

H HARLEQUIN
SPECIAL
EDITION

HARLEQUIN®
SPECIAL
EDITION™

Recycling programs
for this product may
not exist in your area.

ISBN-13: 978-1-335-40820-4

The Cowboy's Christmas Retreat

Copyright © 2021 by Catherine Mann

This edition published by arrangement with Harlequin Books S.A.

For questions and comments about the quality of this book,
please contact us at CustomerService@Harlequin.com.

Harlequin Enterprises ULC
22 Adelaide St. West, 40th Floor
Toronto, Ontario M5H 4E3, Canada
www.Harlequin.com

Printed in U.S.A.

Her gaze shot up from the screen to look at him and she could have sworn an awareness crackled between them.

Surely only because they were both alone, treated poorly by someone who'd vowed to love them forever. As she knew all too well from her ugly breakup, the last thing he needed was anything muddling the recovery.

"No worries," Riley assured her, as if reading her thoughts, those brown eyes of his wise and knowing. "The ranch is family friendly and friend friendly, not just romance. And we are friends, Lucy. You're my best friend."

"And you're mine." She sighed, sagging back onto her heels just as Pickles curled up to sleep beside her. "So, say we're discussing—just discussing— the possibility of me coming with you to spend Christmas at the Top Dog Dude Ranch. It seems unfair to take the trip without contributing. But I can hardly afford a trip to the corner store, much less a two-week vacation. And there's missing work…"

A poor excuse at best, since most of her clients were teachers who would be home for break. She could see that he knew that excuse was thin.

She tried again, unsure why she was resisting when she'd taken so much help from him in the past. Lucy clasped her wrist over where he'd rubbed with his thumb.

Dear Reader,

Welcome to Christmas at the Top Dog Dude Ranch! Christmas has always been my favorite holiday, but it became even more so as I built traditions with my four children. Having such a large family brought Decembers packed with pageants and parties. No doubt, I have stored up plenty of inspiration for a family-focused festive story such as this!

While my kids outgrew some traditions over the years, they clung tightly to others. In particular, they looked forward to attending a living nativity, complete with a petting zoo, hot cocoa and pictures. When my two younger children were in high school, they even invited a crowd of their friends to join us. Those photos were absolutely the best. As I wrote *The Cowboy's Christmas Retreat*, I knew without question that I had to include a living nativity full of Top Dog critters.

Wishing each of you a holiday season of joy and traditions, friendship and love!

Merry Christmas!

Catherine Mann

USA TODAY bestselling author **Catherine Mann** has won numerous awards for her novels, including both a prestigious RITA® Award and an *RT Book Reviews* Reviewers' Choice Award. After years of moving around the country bringing up four children, Catherine has settled in her home state of South Carolina, where she's active in animal rescue. For more information, visit her website, catherinemann.com.

Books by Catherine Mann

Harlequin Special Edition

Top Dog Dude Ranch

Last-Chance Marriage Rescue
The Cowboy's Christmas Retreat

Harlequin Desire

Alaskan Oil Barons

The Baby Claim
The Double Deal
The Love Child
The Twin Birthright
The Second Chance
The Rancher's Seduction
The Billionaire Renegade
The Secret Twin

Texas Cattleman's Club: Houston

Hot Holiday Rancher

Visit the Author Profile page
at Harlequin.com for more titles.

To my children—Brice, Haley, Robbie and Maggie. It's been a joy creating holiday traditions with you!

Chapter One

Lucy Snyder had meant it when she told her ex-husband that her love for him was dead. Nothing killed a relationship like finding out her supposed soul mate had missed the birth of their son because he'd been with another woman.

And now, as she frosted the cake for her child's fourth birthday, she wasn't any less hurt or angry. Just all the more determined not to let the turmoil inside her spoil her little boy's special day.

A special day with a party she was putting together all by herself while her four-year-old ran around the apartment clanging two pots against each other singing the "Little Drummer Boy."

She squeezed the frosting tube, spelling out *G-E-O-R-G-E*. The writing was green, to go with the safari theme for his "wild thing" party. Huffing a hank of hair off her forehead, she willed herself to breathe in, breathe out. But planning a birthday party and planning for Christmas at the same time were kicking her butt.

She'd definitely chosen an appropriate theme for this little guy's party. As she set aside the tube of icing, her gaze caught on her son. He flung back his head to wail the lyrics, his mop of auburn curls shaking, his blue eyes wide. She wanted to give him the world, tough to do on the income from her dog-walking business.

But she was trying her best to create a memorable day that wouldn't be overshadowed by Christmas in a few weeks. At least there wasn't a lot of space to decorate, the apartment small, but all hers, furnished on a shoestring budget when she'd moved here a couple of years ago after her divorce—and how mortifying that she hadn't learned about her ex cheating until her son was two years old? She managed to push back the anger at the betrayal on most days, but George's birthday brought back so many memories.

Except today wasn't about regrets. It was about celebrating George.

In between walking clients' dogs today, she'd decorated her place with green-and-brown balloons and garland. She'd dug through George's toys and placed the animals around the room—an elephant by the pitcher of water. A stuffed tiger crouched under the table. A giraffe looked like it was nibbling on the Christmas tree with twinkling lights and upcycled glass ball ornaments from Donna's Thrift Shop on Center Avenue.

And that fresh tree, cut down just last weekend thanks to her buddy.

A bright spot in an otherwise crazy month—insane day. Her best buddy, Riley Stewart, had come through for her once again, just as he'd done since becoming her best friend in the ninth grade. Riley had been the new kid in school at the start of second semester, a feeling she understood all too well since she'd been new to the school in the middle of first semester.

Their friendship had been cemented over shared crummy cafeteria pizza.

More than once, he'd been there for her, but most of all after her divorce, starting with how he'd let her stay in his apartment while he was out on the rodeo circuit, then helped her move into another apartment in his complex. It had rocked her world to learn about her husband's infidelity, and stung even more that she'd been oblivious for so long. Trust was difficult for her now, most especially trusting her own judgment. But she was going to have to start doing a better job at standing on her own. Riley had his own future to take care of…a future soon to include a wife.

She didn't want to think about how their friendship could be put on the back burner once he got married. Lucy knew the fiancée well enough, and they got along, but who knew how Emily might feel about her husband's friendship with Lucy once the knot was tied?

"Mom. Mom. Mom—"

Her son's voice cut through her thoughts.

"Yes, George?" She swirled the finishing touch on his safari cake. The pastry stand sat ready and waiting thanks to her crafty best bud. During their Christmas tree outing, Riley had sliced circles from another downed tree for her to sand and seal to use as platters. He'd even carved a large number four from a fat branch.

"Mom," George called again, racing past a pile of Legos that would almost certainly lead to massive pain when she accidently stepped on them later. "I know what I want for my birthday. I want a toy garbage truck."

"A toy what?" She leaned back against the counter, licking the red spatula.

"A. Garbage. Truck." He enunciated slowly, banging on the pot once for each word. "The kind that picks up trash. I wanna be a worker man when I grow up and drive that big truck."

"And what else do you want for your birthday?" Hopefully something that she'd already bought and wrapped so he wouldn't be disappointed. Her budget was tapped out. A tightness gripped her chest as she looked at the neat pile of birthday presents on the only-slightly used pine coffee table at the center of her living area.

"Just a garbage truck. That's all." Another clang echoed as George resumed playing his song, moving around the well-worn sofa, nearly tripping over the tan-and-red geometric rug. Both the rug and sofa were finds from Donna's Thrift Shop, something she'd been proud to purchase to make her son's life better. He beat the pots a few more times before dropping them to the ground.

The sound reverberated through the two-bedroom apartment and she prayed Mr. Whelan downstairs wouldn't complain to the manager again. She'd done everything to make their future as bright as the twinkling silver tinsel on the fireplace mantel.

Kicking aside the pot, George started racing around the apartment, making truck noises. He continued on his "route," circling the fat leather sofa, careening into the coat tree full of dog leashes. Their scruffy little border terrier mix—Pickles—bounced up off his fluffy bed and joined the chase with all fifteen pounds of canine energy.

"Garbage truck," George announced. "Vroom. Vroom. Beep. Beep."

Sadly, this was the first she'd heard of his fascination with waste disposal, so it wasn't reflected in any of the gifts for his birthday. "If you don't get the truck for your birthday, then maybe you'll get it from Santa."

"Or Dad will get it for me."

Her stomach sank and she flung the spatula in the sink. Her heart broke all over again because she couldn't give her child the things his dad did.

"You'll have to ask him, but he may have already bought your presents." Although he would likely buy it anyway.

Colin had gone overboard in spoiling George when they were together and doubled down on the extravagance afterward. There was no way she could have kept up, even if she was still a veterinary technician.

After the divorce, she'd quickly used up her vacation days with George's chronic ear infections. When Riley had connected her with a dog-walking job, she'd leaped at the opportunity for work with more flexibility. She was even able to bring George in his stroller.

She wanted to cry out with frustration at her ex-husband for refusing to help with childcare. She would have had to take him back to court to change the custody agreement and she didn't have the money. A catch-22.

But she held the anger inside. For George's sake, she worked her tail off at peaceful coparenting. Even when Colin refused to attend his kid's birthday party. He'd said he would just wait to celebrate when he picked up George for his part of Christmas vacation.

"George, honey, please be careful not to knock over the tree. I don't want you to get hurt." She needed to take him to the playground, but his snowsuit was in the dryer and his little friends were due to show up in four hours. What had she been thinking planning a party in her tiny apartment in December with Kentucky temperatures below freezing? Maybe if she lived in Southern Florida. But Southern Kentucky? Nope.

"Garbage man, here for pick up, ma'am." George lifted a small waste basket and tossed in two wooden coasters, then a fistful of crayons and a snow boot. He zoomed to Lucy and screeched to a halt. "Garbage man, here for pick up. Do you have any trash for me, pretty lady?"

He looked so earnest she couldn't hold back a smile. She grabbed a pile of napkins off the counter, wadded them up and threw them into the bin. "There you go. Thank you so much." She dropped a quick kiss onto his head, tousling his red curls. "I'm so glad my home will be clean for my sweet son's birthday party. Have you seen him? He needs to change into clean clothes pretty soon."

"I'll tell him." He backpedaled, stumbled, then righted himself into that gravity-defying way of children that kept her living in a constant state of fear of the next tumble.

She rubbed her hands along her tie-dyed sweatshirt, smearing frosting, already exhausted. But she was afraid to look away for even a moment and miss a milestone—or a catastrophe. He was all motion.

"When does Daddy come to my party?"

She winced. "You're having a party at your father's house over Christmas. Remember?"

"But I could call him. I want him to come to my safari party. He's gonna come."

"I don't think so." It broke her heart on a regular basis seeing the way her child chased after his daddy, only to have him cancel or reschedule visits constantly. So, she'd also meant it when she'd told her ex she didn't care if she ever saw him again. But George *did* want to see him.

Her eyes stung and the ringing in her ears grew so loud she almost missed the sound of her son crashing into the Christmas tree. Ornaments rained to the ground. Lights slid off, wrapping around George until he and the tree were one.

Her heart in her throat, she sprinted across the apartment. She dropped to her knees, skimming her hands over George as he gulped in big gasps of air, tears streaming down his face. He looked okay, just scared.

But what if…?

"George, where does it hurt?"

He was her world. Her everything.

She would do anything to keep him safe and happy. "Tell Mommy where it hurts and I'll kiss the boo-boo, okay?"

"I'm okay. But my cake isn't." Blue eyes widened as he pointed behind her.

She looked over her shoulder and… Oh no.

Pickles was on the counter, face buried in the middle of the cake.

* * *

A bloodcurdling shriek split the air.

Riley bolted from the elevator, recognizing that scream all too well. The same scream Lucy had let loose the one and only time he'd managed to get her to ride a horse.

He hoped this shout didn't end in stitches.

Charging ahead past his apartment to hers, he embraced the distraction from the mess he'd made of his own life. He rang the doorbell once as a courtesy only, before pulling out his key to her place. He pushed the door open to…mayhem.

Pickles was running in circles, barking up a storm. George sat in the middle of a pile of Christmas tree lights and ornaments, tinsel in his red curls. Lucy scooped up the dog, both of them covered in frosting. Tears sheened in her green eyes as Pickles licked icing from her cheek.

Her chin quivered.

Oh man. He wrapped her in a hug, his chin resting on the top of her head. "What happened, Lucy?"

"Nothing. I'm fine." Dog smooshed between them, she held on tight, whispering against his chest in a rambling litany. "I don't want George to see me upset. He knocked over the tree and I thought he was hurt, but he's okay and Pickles ate half of the cake and I don't have time or ingredients to make another one and—"

"Okay, Lucy. Take a moment to step back and catch your breath. I've got this." He took Pickles from her, the back of his hand brushing her breast.

He froze. Her eyes shot up to his. Pink crept up her cheeks until her freckles almost disappeared.

A surprise bolt of awareness sizzled through him. And just that fast he was blindsided by a deluge of sensations: the scent of Lucy's wavy red hair, the soft feel of her body. A whiff of her cinnamon perfume.

Sure, he'd harbored a crush on her long ago, but it was just that. An infatuation. He valued her friendship too much to risk acting on something as transient as sex.

Her breath hitched and she stepped back, her throat moving in a gulp. "Thanks. I think you're right. I should, uh, clean the frosting off myself."

She backed toward the bathroom, tugging nervously at the hem of her tie-dyed sweatshirt, smudging more frosting on her black leggings, her bare toes curling against the rug. She spun fast and disappeared into the bathroom.

"Mommy said a bad word."

Riley shook off whatever it was that had zipped between him and Lucy. It had to be because of all the crazy accusations Emily had hurled at him to justify why she was leaving him for another guy. Wedding off. Honeymoon canceled. He hung his fleece-lined jacket on the coat tree and turned to George.

"Well, tiger, your mom probably just slipped up. We all make mistakes sometimes." He'd made a whopper of an error in choosing to propose to a woman only interested in the size of a rodeo champ's belt buckle. "How about we start clearing away some of this mess before your mom comes back?"

He worked methodically, untangling, setting the world to rights again, grateful to restore order in this realm at least. Much preferable to thinking about the fact that his fiancée had dumped him. They'd fought over dinner the night before and he'd hoped to repair things in the morning. Only to walk in on her with her new boyfriend.

Or maybe he was an old boyfriend.

Finding them in the middle of a lip-lock, he hadn't been the least bit interested in hearing details. He'd left and headed straight for the one person he'd always been able to rely on.

Lucy. His rock since the ninth grade.

The hum of the bathroom fan halted as the white door creaked open. Lucy stepped out in fresh leggings and a simple long sweater. Barefoot, she stood no more than five foot two inches, the same height she'd been in the ninth grade. And no matter how many times she assured him she could hold her own, he couldn't tamp down the urge to protect her.

"Thank you for being here, yet again, to clean up the mess in my life. You can taste test for me as my way of saying thanks." She nodded toward the sugar cookies. "I made plenty so we can decorate the extras for Christmas."

He steeled himself to stifle a wince over the mention of the holidays. He'd never been much of a fan of the season after having spent too many hiding in his room when his father got high.

"I can pick up one of those premade cakes or some cupcakes." He waved at the tiny plastic animals on the counter. "You can put those on top. It's all okay."

"Do you think there's a garbage-truck cake anywhere in this town?" Lucy chewed her lip, a habit she'd had as long as they'd been friends. A universal signal that something was off in her world.

"Uhm, run that by me again?"

She swept her hands under her eyes and shot him a bright, brave grin. "He wants a toy garbage truck for his birthday. I bought him a little police car. How did I not hear what he really prefers?"

"He changes his mind daily. He's a kid. That's what they do. My nieces were all about dolls last week and now they're bananas for art supplies."

She strode over to the Christmas tree and picked up the lights. Her scruffy little dog followed, tail wagging. "I can't afford for him to change his mind."

He reached toward his coat, still dripping with melting snow. "I'll make the trip to the store quick so I'm back in time to help—"

"No. But thank you. I wasn't hinting. You already do so much for us." She pressed her lips together tightly for a moment before continuing, "I guess I'm most upset that I can't be the one to get it for him."

He picked up the tree and righted it in the stand. "You're his mom. He loves you. No amount of gifts will change that."

"Thanks. I'm better now. Really." She draped the lights back in place branch by branch. "I'll walk with him all around the neighborhood on trash day so he can see the real deal close up."

Kneeling, he scooped up a wooden puppy paw ornament. His hand skimmed the rug, knuckles coming into contact with the soft fibers. He was constantly amazed at all she'd done to create this new life for herself and George in such a short amount of time.

"You're a great mother. George knows that he's loved."

"I appreciate your saying that. And I really mean it that we don't need a cake. I can just glob extra frosting on one of the cookies and stick a candle in it. The kids can put the small plastic animals on their cookies. It'll be fine." She took an ornament from him. "Enough about me. What brought you here early?"

Scooping up an ornament with George's name, Riley used the excuse to duck his head to hide the hurt in his eyes that he knew she would see too easily. Lucy always could read him.

"We can talk about that later. Give me your list for the grocery store. Cupcakes and what else?"

"Riley? Thanks. Again. But I mean it when I say no." She reached to touch his arm to stop him, then pulled back. "What's going on? You're upset about something. I can tell."

He didn't want to burden her with his own problems when she already had so much on her plate. But he found it impossible to refuse those emerald-colored eyes when she looked at him that way. He knew she wouldn't relent until she'd chased the answer out of him. He huffed out a defeated breath.

"Emily and I are over."

Her eyes went wide. "What? But you're getting married at Christmas."

"We most assuredly are not." He exhaled hard, his cheeks puffing. "She was quite clear last night." Vocal and loud, heaping all sorts of accusations on his head as to why it was somehow his fault she'd landed in bed with another man.

"Couples fight. Surely she didn't mean it."

Images flashed in his head of Emily with her arms wrapped around another man. The betrayal hadn't hurt as much as he knew it should have, his pride stinging more than his heart.

"She was crystal clear. She doesn't want to get married—not to me, at least."

"I'm so sorry. What reason did she give?"

Pickles circled twice under the tree, tucking his legs under so he was in a tight ball beside George. Riley measured his words, not sure how to explain that Emily was jealous of his friendship with Lucy. There had never been a romantic moment between them as adults—and only one impulsive kiss in high school. Lucy was beautiful, no question, but he knew how badly she'd been treated by her ex and the last thing she needed or wanted was some- one toying with her heart.

"She said I didn't really love her." Avoiding her

knowing eyes, he picked up a snowflake ornament and placed it on a high bough.

George came barreling over, lifting his stuffed dog to a space between a car ornament and a maca-roni tree ornament George made last year.

"Why in the world would she think that? Everyone knows you two are in love." Lucy snagged a metal ornament shaped like Kentucky, securing it on a tree branch closer to the ground. A Christmas light shone through the hole in the ornament marking their town of Middlesboro.

"Apparently not. I found her making out with another man this morning—someone I know from the rodeo circuit."

"Riley, I'm sorry." She touched his arm, no pulling back this time, and squeezed. Firmly. "She doesn't deserve you."

He scrubbed his hand through his hair. "I'm sorry for laying all of this on you when you're in the middle of getting ready for the party."

"You have nothing to apologize for. You've been there for me more times than I can even count."

"Lucy, you know it's my honor."

"Thank you." She held up a hand to stop him. "Today is about George. I just love him so much and it seems like no matter how hard I try to make this day special, I keep messing it up."

"George is going to have a wonderful time. Don't you worry about that for a minute."

She laid her hand on her son's shoulder, a sweet, maternal gesture. And Riley wanted to be there for her. She deserved so much better than the stress and problems her ex had heaped on her. So did George, for that matter. Lucy and George meant the world to him, and they needed him. He regretted putting so much time into his relationship with Emily, a relationship that had only bit him in the butt, whereas Lucy had always been there for him.

And just like that, he found himself saying the last thing he would have expected, but words that felt one-hundred-percent right. "Speaking of having a wonderful time... I was wondering if you would like to go with me on my honeymoon?"

Chapter Two

"Honeymoon? Together? No disrespect, my dear friend, but have you lost your mind?" Lucy searched his deep brown eyes and found them as steady as ever.

"I've already paid for the two weeks at the Top Dog Dude Ranch." He clapped a hand to his chest in earnest. "It would be a shame to see it go to waste."

Riley's jaw tightened just a hint. Almost imperceptible. But Lucy knew this look well. The sharpening of his square jaw first emerged the day he confided in her when his high school girlfriend dumped him a week before senior prom.

Her shock now shifted to something softer, to concern. Because he was hurting and she'd been too wrapped up in herself and her own worries to see he had something far bigger going on in his world right now. What kind of friend did that make her? Not a good one. She'd leaned on his broad and capable shoulders far too often.

She glanced at her son to make sure he was occupied so she was free to focus and found George had abandoned picking up his toys. He lay on his stomach under the tree, Pickles curled up asleep beside him.

Turning back to Riley, she sat cross-legged on the floor, taking his hands in hers, sad for him and so very angry at Emily for hurting this amazing man.

"Riley, that's a generous offer, but we couldn't possibly accept. I realize you already terminated your lease on your apartment…" Something that made her stomach knot. She'd grown used to having him so close and that wasn't fair to him. "You know you're welcome to stay here with us. George will be thrilled to have you around more, not even having to walk out into the hall and go a few doors down. George can sleep on a cot in my room. You can stay in his room. Or out here on the sofa bed. Just for the holiday."

Did he know he was rubbing the insides of her wrists with his thumbs? Although it wasn't unusual for him to take her hands. So why did it feel really nice today?

"That's my point, Lucy. If we're going to spend the holiday *together*, why not make use of a vacation? George would enjoy himself."

Now *that* was a move guaranteed to gain traction with her. Except for one point...

"But Riley, you know I'm terrified of horses. Don't you think that sort of vacation would be wasted on me?"

And not for the first time, she thought about the irony of her fear of horses and how she'd studied to be a vet tech. Although she'd fast realized during training that her specialty was the smaller animals. Basically, the kind under four hundred pounds that didn't fling her into a creek. Her dog-walking business suited her.

He shook his head, a thick lock of dark brown hair sliding over his brow. "The Top Dog Dude Ranch is about much more than just horses—although that's certainly a draw for me. The place focuses more on helping people grow closer. It's about lifting spirits and healing hearts."

"Well, then you would most certainly get your money's worth with you and me," she said wryly.

Releasing her hands, he chuckled and she couldn't help but join in. They'd always been able to make each other laugh even when life was falling apart. He pulled his phone from his faded jeans and typed in a search for the ranch's website. "Here. Check this out."

She cupped her hand over his on the cell, his skin warm. Familiar. And affecting her in a way that scrambled her thoughts at the worst time.

Clearing her throat, she read from the cell screen, "'Welcome to Moonlight Ridge, Tennessee, home to the Top Dog Dude Ranch, renowned for family-friendly rustic retreats that heal broken hearts. Some say it's the majestic mountain vistas. Others vow there's magic in the hot springs. All agree, there's something special about the four-legged creatures at Top Dog Dude Ranch that give guests a "new leash on love."'"

New leash on love? Had Riley known on some level his marriage would already need bolstering?

Her gaze shot up from the screen to look at him and she could have sworn an awareness crackled between them. Surely only because they were both alone, treated poorly by someone who'd vowed to love them forever. As she knew all too well from her ugly breakup, the last thing he needed was anything muddling the recovery.

"No worries," he assured her as if reading her thoughts, those brown eyes of his wise and knowing. "The ranch is family friendly and friend friendly, not just romance. And we are friends, Lucy. You're my best friend."

"And you're mine." She sighed, sagging back onto her heels just as Pickles curled up to sleep beside her. "So, say we're discussing—just discussing—the possibility of me coming with you to spend Christmas at the Top Dog Dude Ranch. It seems unfair to take the trip without contributing. But I can hardly afford a trip to the corner store, much less a two-week vacation. And there's missing work..."

A poor excuse at best since most of her clients were teachers who would be home for break. She could see that he knew that excuse was thin.

She tried again, unsure why she was resisting when she'd taken so much help from him in the past. Lucy clasped her wrist over where he'd rubbed with his thumb. "George goes to his father's Christmas Eve night."

"His dad can pick him up there." He dispensed with her excuse easily enough. "It's not any farther for him to drive than coming here."

He had a point. The ranch in Moonlight Ridge

was outside of Gatlinburg, not too horribly far away from their town of Middlesboro, Kentucky.

"You've thought of everything." As always. "It truly is such a generous offer."

"You really would be doing me a favor," he said, his brown eyes somber. "I won't be alone at Christmas. I need you, my friend."

Just that fast all of her objections melted away at his words, the ones guaranteed to reel her in. Riley needed her. And as he was always there for her, she had to figure out a way to do the same. "Let me think about it."

Six hours later, Riley dropped into his recliner. He twisted the top off a beer bottle and knocked back a swig before scrolling through his cell phone for the number for the Top Dog Dude Ranch's owner. While Lucy hadn't officially agreed to come with him, he knew her well and he was hopeful. It was just a matter of time, as long as he gave her the space to think things through. She would go with him for her son, if nothing else, and he would take that win however it came.

Truth be told, he looked forward to showering the kid with all the fun the Tennessee ranch had to offer. Riley didn't have any nieces or nephews to shower. But he'd been a part of George's life from day one, the first visitor to see the little tyke, then each of George's birthdays ever since, including today's shindig. Riley's ears were still ringing from the "wild thing" bash that only grew wilder the more frosting the kids slathered on their sugar cookies. Lucy's tears and worries had been unneeded.

His hand clenched around the phone as he found the number he'd searched for—Jacob O'Brien. He'd learned about the Top Dog Dude Ranch when O'Brien had placed some grazing land in upstate Kentucky for sale in order to finance an expansion of his ranch. Riley had been searching for land for a horse farm, ready to settle down and start a family of his own.

Little had he known that would actually be the final nail in the coffin to his dreams of domestic bliss, leaving him stuck in an apartment of empty walls and packing boxes. Merry Christmas.

Taking another swallow of beer, he pushed back a fresh surge of anger at Emily as the cell call went through.

"Hello?" Jacob O'Brien's voice came over the speaker phone. "I hope all's well with you and the wedding plans."

Riley stifled a wince, staring hard at a half-packed box of towels. "Thanks, but I have a request regarding my reservation. Not a cancellation. Just a change."

"Anything. Just say the word and I'll make it happen. This is the Christmas season, after all."

Although there was no sign of the holidays in his apartment other than a piece of artwork on his refrigerator—a Christmas tree made out of George's handprints, a preschool project he'd proudly passed to Riley. Lord, he loved that little guy.

He scratched a thumb along the writing on his beer bottle. "I need to make some changes."

"How so?"

As grateful as he was to have the engagement end rather than have a broken marriage, he was still embarrassed. He took a swig of the craft brew before forging ahead. "My engagement is off and there's no chance of reconciliation. I have a friend accompanying me to the ranch instead."

"My friend, I'm sorry to hear that. I can refund your money, no problem. We have a waiting list."

"Actually, I need to get away. This friend doesn't get much in the way of vacations, so it seems like a good idea to bring her." At least he hoped she would be accompanying him. He didn't intend to give up.

"You don't think you'll be upset visiting here and thinking of your plan with Emily?"

He was surprised at the man's question, but then

they had gotten to know each other better during the negotiations over purchasing the farmland. And the question was valid—but not an issue. Riley's gaze slid to where Emily usually sat in this apartment. All that almost was—a lifetime of her laughter, smiles and coconut-scented perfume—now gone. The thought of spending Christmas in this graveyard of the future seized his chest.

"Not at all. Lucy will help me exorcise any thoughts of my ex." He looked around his apartment, corners full of boxes readying for his move he'd expected to make after returning from his honeymoon. He'd even terminated his lease. He might well end up sleeping on Lucy's sofa after all if he didn't get his life together.

"Fair enough then. I'll have your place ready for you and your friend Lucy."

Something in the man's tone made Riley rush to add, "Lucy will be bringing her four-year-old son, so we'll need a cot in the cabin."

His honeymoon special had only called for a king-size bed, not that he would be sleeping there. He was bound for a holiday of sofa sleeping.

"Ah right. George, isn't he?" Jacob had a way of remembering all the small details of the folks he interacted with. That was a part of what made him such a successful businessman.

And what a time to realize how much he'd gone on and on about the kid, like George was his… Riley cut the thought short.

"Yea. Thanks for understanding. One last thing, I'm going to be mailing a garbage truck to put under the tree in our cabin…"

Lucy pulled a platter from the dishwasher, her third load since the party, but she'd had the bright idea to save money by not buying paper plates.

She would likely end up spending more on water, power and detergent. Riley had offered to stay and help, but she needed some time alone to organize her thoughts. Which would have been impossible to manage with his big, hulking self around.

Not to mention the unsettling sound of her ex-husband's voice coming through her son's tablet as the two FaceTimed a birthday call.

Bare feet pressed into the orange-and-red mandala rug, she curled her toes into the soft texture comforting her as she pulled the faded reindeer dish towel from its place hanging on the gas stove. Mess billowed all around her—plates and mugs with the afterlife of cookies and hot cocoa. How nine people had managed to produce such chaos never ceased to blow her mind.

Admittedly, the dishwasher had seen better

years. The device still cleaned dishes fine. Drying, however, was a different story altogether. Pulling a green platter from the dishwasher, she made quick work of drying.

The kitchen window was framed in a soft white glow from string lights, a wreath in the center made from greenery on her tree-cutting outing with Riley. Lucy tried her best to keep an eye on George as he zipped around the living room with his tablet while zoning out from the conversation with his dad.

The tactic was doomed, though. Her attention was pulled in by Colin's voice.

"Happy birthday, son. Did you have a good party?"

Heel pivoting to the cabinet behind her, Lucy struggled for something—anything—else to focus on other than thinking of all the ways Colin had cheated George by being a less-than-honorable man. She zeroed in on a mundane distraction. Like straightening the community of mismatched plates in the cabinet, an eclectic set of different colors. She'd grown to love the cobbled-together nature of her life since her life fell apart.

"I had a great party. I'm a 'wild thing'!" He danced around the room. "I got a police car and dinosaurs and superheroes and a light-up gauntlet that flashes green, blue, yellow. And Riley got me a sled for the snow. He said he's gonna take me tomorrow down a big hill behind our apartment building."

"Sounds like you raked it in, pal. Talia has planned another birthday party with all her nieces and nephews after Christmas."

Not for the first time, Lucy wished the apartment was larger, so she didn't have to hear every detail of these calls. She wanted George to be happy, to have fun and be celebrated. At least she could take comfort in the fact Colin hadn't married the woman he'd cheated with. Small comfort. She just prayed he wouldn't cheat on Talia, too, because then George's world would be upended again and that's the last thing she wanted.

Her child needed—deserved—stability.

And as for the extra birthday party at his father's? She appreciated the effort, but George didn't know any of those nieces and nephews. He would have preferred having his father here with people who were familiar to him.

"Dad, Dad, Dad, be sure to tell Santa Claus where I'll be. Promise?"

"Yes, son, I absolutely will. Talia and I have big plans for you. We're going to go see ZooLights and take family photos—"

Whatever else he listed was drowned out by the roaring in her ears. Family pictures? She knew intellectually that they were all a blended family, but hearing that her son would be in a Christmas "family" photo that didn't include her? That cut her to the core.

Breathing in the scent of the vanilla-cookie candle on the counter, she sagged back and looked at the collection of framed pictures on the fireplace mantel. Photographs of George as an infant. The start of the family she'd believed she was creating. The way George's soft features and wisps of red hair stirred an emotion in her so deep and ancient that love was an inadequate container.

Did Colin feel the same depth of emotion? She hoped so. George deserved it and she wanted the best for her kid. So, she tried, however she could, to put her own anger at Colin aside and help her little one bond with his dad. She'd placed photos of George and Colin together in her son's bedroom. Pictures of outings they'd shared. Her gaze slid to another image…one of Riley and George with matching baseball mitts.

George squealed, juggling the tablet around so much that most likely only half his face showed. "And, Dad, you won't forget to have cookies for Santa? Promise?"

"What kind do you want?"

"Sugar cookies. They're my favorite." He turned fast, toward the kitchen, and dropped the tablet on the counter. "Here's Mommy. I gotta play."

She glanced at the tablet with about as much enthusiasm as she would stare down a reptile. Then, pasting on a neutral expression, she retrieved the device from beside the leftover cookies. "Hi, Colin, uhm, thanks for making sure he has a wonderful Christmas."

Was it catty to be glad he was dying his hair?

"He's a great kid. You're doing a good job with him."

He grinned with a charm that had once wooed her into believing in forever. She was wiser now.

"So, uh, I may have a slight change to the plan, and I'd like to run it past you to see what you think."

His smile faded, his blue eyes flashing with a quick rise of temper. "Now listen, Lucy, I'm not giving up Christmas with him. It's my year, as per the custody agreement." He shoved a hand through his thinning blond hair. "My next-door neighbor warned me this easy exchange was too good to be true."

And just that fast, she was absolutely certain about taking Riley up on his offer. George deserved the fun, and so did she, especially since she was facing Christmas without her child. "Colin. Calm down. The holiday hand-off date is as agreed. I just need to adjust where you pick him up."

She was going to the Top Dog Dude Ranch for a cowboy Christmas.

Two weeks later, Riley draped his wrist over the steering wheel as he drove along the narrow road through the Smoky Mountains on his way to the Top Dog Dude Ranch. Snow drifted from the sky as if ordered just for the holiday. Lucy's minivan was packed to the gills with suitcases, toys and gifts.

Minivan.

He would have preferred his truck with its four-wheel drive, but there hadn't been enough room for all of their stuff, even with a king cab. Lucy had reminded him that they weren't just packing for a regular trip, but also for Christmas. Plus, everything needed to keep a four-year-old entertained in the car and in the cabin.

George had been reluctant to leave any of his new birthday toys at home. Wearing his puffy blue jacket with his gloves attached to the sleeves, he had his backpack beside him and a bucket of Legos at his feet.

Pickles sat in the other seat in his doggy seat

belt, snoring lightly. Thank goodness the place allowed for guests to bring their personal dogs. They just had to send vet records and agree to keep the dog on leash at all times when outside.

Christmas carols played over the radio. Down in the valley, colored lights twinkled on houses in the dusk. Ice on bare branches shimmered.

He hated the Christmas season.

Too much hearing about everyone's happy holiday memories and too few of his own. His mom dead and his dad using that as an excuse to seek out another fix, and another, chased with whatever alcohol Riley hadn't been able to find and pour out. Christmas his ninth grade year, right before their move, his dad had seemed level for once and insisted they go shopping. He'd told Riley to pick out whatever he wanted.

His dad had shoved the electronic game into Riley's backpack. He hadn't known until the security alarm went off on their way out of the store. His father had gotten the guard to let them go by promising to punish his "thieving" son.

That was the year Riley had stopped believing his old man's garbage. And he'd stopped believing in holiday cheer. He'd hoped to change that with a Christmas wedding. At least Lucy had helped him salvage something from these next two weeks and he was determined to make the most of it.

Starting today.

Lucy flipped through the pages in their registration packet, reviewing the amenities and activities the ranch had to offer. She'd shut down her phone half an hour ago when cell service grew spotty. "George, there are all sorts of things for us to do like a Christmas parade of boats and a petting zoo that's a nativity. They also have reindeer rides and horse rides."

Riley saw the corner of her mouth flicker and he angled closer. "Are you sure I couldn't convince you to give horseback riding one more try? I'm a much better teacher now."

The minivan took the snowy roads in stride as Riley guided them toward a covered wooden bridge with tall, angled steeples from well-aged pine that framed the little tunnel. But for Riley, the vague stable-like shape doubled down on his recollection of Lucy from yesteryear. She'd been all white knuckles and terrified screams on Patches, a usually well-mannered Appaloosa mare who should have been an easy ride. He really wanted to overlay that memory since Lucy deserved better.

She shook her head, a lock of red hair sliding loose as she laughed softly. "I'll be by the fire reading a book, drinking a cup of cider and keeping my feet toasty warm."

He laughed just as George chimed in. "Reindeer rides? Will we be able to see Santa too? I can ask him for a garbage truck."

Lucy twisted in her seat to answer. "It says here that there are plenty of opportunities to talk to Santa."

Riley glanced into the rearview mirror making eye contact with George in the back, his legs swinging as he bumped his snow boots against the seat. "What do you think Santa Claus should bring to your mommy?"

From the rearview mirror, Riley watched George's face scrunch up in thought as he stared out the window toward the snow-filled woods.

"A new leash for the dogs?"

"That's a good idea. But what about something for her when she's not at work? Maybe you and I could go shopping together when we get there."

"Yeah, that'd be great. I'm gonna draw my list." He dug into his backpack.

Riley glanced at Lucy sitting curled in her seat, with her messy bun, Lucy's "I overslept" signature look, and the expression which always tugged her pink lips upward into a faint smile… So cute.

He'd been right to invite her. She would help

him salvage something from this abysmal holiday. He just had to keep things light, because he was too sad about his ex. And Lucy had been reluctant about the trip anyway.

"So, Lucy," Riley said. "Have you been a good girl this year or have you been naughty?"

Chapter Three

Nice or…naughty?

Struggling to keep her jaw from dropping, Lucy studied Riley, his innuendo-laden question hanging in the air between them. Was he trying to be funny? They always teased each other. Why should today be any different?

They were only going to spend two weeks alone together in a cabin. A honeymoon cabin. Both of them completely unattached for one of the rare times in their friendship.

And they would be alone-alone once George went to his dad's until after the New Year.

She tipped her chin and said in her very best

"friend" voice, "You can tell Santa Claus that I have been the very nicest of girls this year."

"I'll be sure he gets the memo. Or you can tell him yourself at one of his visits to the dude ranch." He eased off the gas, slowing to take an icy turn with care. "Speaking of which, did you remember to pack an obnoxious Christmas sweater for the ugly sweater party?"

"I found one with a grumpy pug on it that says Bah Hum Pug. I bought it yesterday afternoon." She'd had so many things to pick up yesterday, poor George had fallen asleep in the shopping cart.

"Yesterday?" He frowned. "You're not usually one to put things off until the last minute."

She curled her toes in her boots, stretching her legs to get her feet closer toes the heater's blast. "I didn't want to spend the money if you changed your mind about the trip."

He lifted an eyebrow. "Why would I do that?"

"If you and Emily reconciled." Her stomach knotted over the possibility of the woman hurting Riley again. She swallowed hard, focusing on the flutter of snow that continued to gather and grow outside.

"Trust me," he said tightly. "There's no chance of that. None at all."

She hadn't seen him this quietly crushed since

his dad emptied Riley's bank account and blew it on drugs. She looked back at her son to make sure he wasn't listening and found he was flipping through a storybook, pretending to read it to Pickles. The scruffy pup's head rested gently on the edge of the car seat. His little pink tongue lolled out to the side.

Turning back to Riley, she kept her voice low. "Are you ready to talk about it?"

"I already told you what happened." His fists went white knuckled around the steering wheel.

"The basics. A few lines." She touched his arm tentatively, only a brief brush before pulling back. That slight, strange crackle of *something* filling her awareness again. "There's always more to anything this big, though."

He shot her a half grin mixed with a grimace. "She swears it was just the one time."

"Do you believe her?"

How easy it would be to simply skewer Emily. But she owed it to Riley to try to stay objective and support his decision either way. And yes, maybe there was a part of her that worried if she badmouthed Emily and then Riley made up with her, Lucy could lose his friendship for good.

"That doesn't matter either way. Once was enough. So that's it for me when it comes to a relationship with Emily." His words rang with unmistakable conviction.

While she was sad that he had to feel this way at all, at least she wouldn't have to pretend to like someone who cheated on Riley. "Why now, though? This close to the wedding?"

"Because my plans for the farm are going so well, I'm devoting myself to that full-time."

After visiting the land and weighing in on the design for the new barn, Lucy knew this was a great plan for his future that could expand far beyond rodeo days. "I'm still not following how that ties into problems with Emily."

"She hoped I would change my mind about the farm because she wanted the excitement of being with a rodeo champ, not the day-to-day toil of being married to a horse rancher."

"I'm sorry. I never would have thought she would be so shallow." She rushed to add, "That was rude of me to say. I just can't help but be angry at her for hurting you that way."

He shrugged. "She knows what she wants and I know what life I want. It's as simple as that."

"You don't have to put on a brave front for me."

She watched his expression carefully, trying to read him. He'd always been handsome. But now Riley wore his maturity well with a chiseled jawline that did not yield to years and broken promises.

"Here it is. Straight up. I'm embarrassed. Angry. But not crushed in the way I should be." His gaze flicked back to the road, the van slowing down as the snow and brake lights intensified. "I can't bring myself to judge her for leaving when maybe I wasn't as all-in as I should have been."

Well, that sure sounded definite. She exhaled a sigh of relief that she could finally open up about her feelings on the subject. "That's magnanimous of you to say. But you'll pardon me if I can't let her off the hook as easily. If she wanted to break things off, she should have done it before lining up another guy."

"Thank you. I appreciate your indignation on my behalf." He tugged a stray lock of her red hair. "Here you are coming through for me again, just like in high school when my date bailed before prom."

"We had fun, no relationship pressure." She tucked her hair behind her ear. "Just friends dancing until they closed the place down."

Both of them ignoring that just before the dance, they'd kissed. Unplanned. Unexpected. Unforgettable.

She cleared her throat and chased away the

memory of something they'd vowed never to repeat. Hiding her face, she reached for her tote bag on the floor. "Uhm, I'm going to check over our reservation again."

Riley drummed his fingers on the steering wheel, the only sounds the slap of the windshield wipers swishing away snow and the rustle of Lucy turning another page in her megabinder full of vacation plans. Even George was asleep.

The car ride should have only been a couple of hours, but the snowy conditions had slowed them to a crawl. Not to mention, it felt longer with the uncomfortable discussion about Emily's defection and the weight of his failure on his shoulders.

Lucy flipped another page. He'd asked her once why she didn't just store it all in her cell phone. She'd looked at him like he was crazy and listed all the reasons that data could be lost. Physical notes were her fail-proof backup—the reason for her three shelves filled with old notebooks.

Smiling at the thought, he honed his focus on the road. Wind tunneled through the mountains, turns tight, the road hugging along a rock wall. Then the road narrowed while the trees parted to reveal a retreat so perfect it could have been straight from a

Christmas card. Signs shaped like paw prints directed him to the Top Dog Dude Ranch.

Closer and closer, he drove toward the cluster of cabins with smoking chimneys nestled into the mountainside behind the stately main lodge that sprawled like a sort of rustic castle nestled in the foothills of towering mountains. Bright warm lights encircled a fat pine. A red barn and what looked to be incredible stables waited off to the side. Thank goodness he had Lucy and George to share these two weeks with and salvage something of the season.

"Oh my," Lucy gasped. "That's absolutely stunning. George? George, sweetie, wake up. Look."

She juggled her notebook and reached back to pat her son's leg softly. He jolted awake, rubbed his eyes and stretched his head…then…

"Whoa, look," he squealed. "It's Santa's house."

Laughing softly, she pulled out her cell. "I have an email that indicates our cabin will be ready in an hour. They sent a list of easy activities to choose from if we arrive early."

"Why don't you ask George what he wants to do?" He steered into the parking lot, tires crunching through the snow and ice.

Notebook open again, she thumbed through

pages until settling on the right one. "Well, they have cookies with Santa and—"

"Yes," George chimed in, dropping his water bottle on the floor. "I want that."

"And reindeer rides," Lucy added as he drove slowly past the line of parked cars with license plates from around the country, even one from Canada.

"I want *that*," George squealed, drumming his booted feet against the seat. "Rudolph rides. Rudolph rides."

Slowing the van to let a couple carrying a little dog carrier cross, Riley scouted an empty spot a few yards from the front of the lodge.

Lucy tapped her binder. "And train tours with Santa as the conductor."

"That. That. That!" George shouted, trying to put on his gloves. "I want train rides."

Chuckling, Riley eased into the empty spot. "So, Lucy, what would you like to do while we wait?"

She peered up from her notes to take in the scenery, the reflection from the decorative white lights making her red hair glow a fiery auburn. "The train ride with Santa gives us a tour of the ranch. That may help us choose our schedule for other days."

Riley nodded, putting the minivan in Park and turning off the engine. "A train ride it is then."

While Lucy unbuckled George and made sure he had on his mittens, Riley lifted Pickles out and set him on the ground for a quick walk around on the leash. The shaggy little fella looked so darn cute in his plaid sweater and doggie booties as he sniffed around the new locale. His ears twitched at the sound of a horse whinnying in the distance. Then his puppy tail wagged in excitement.

George was jumping up and down, tugging left and right trying to get a better view. Not that Riley could blame him.

The place was everything Riley had expected and more. From the stables to the lodge, to the horses and other livestock so seamlessly blended into the activity. And all the dog-themed signs and activities were just right for Lucy. Her gift with handling dogs was beyond compare.

"Hey, George," Riley called, "would you like to ride on my shoulders so you can see everything while we make our way over to the train?"

"Yes, please." He extended his arms.

Riley passed the leash to Lucy, careful not to let their hands brush after those moments of awareness earlier. And how strange was that? Their friendship had been…just that. A friendship. He resented this awkwardness between them that threatened what they had.

Hopefully, this snow-enveloped landscape would set everything in his life right. And the first step to that level of normalcy? Greeting the owner of Top Dog Dude Ranch and his wife.

This first objective seemed achievable as the front porch came into view complete with two people he recognized from the brochure. A man and woman both with dark hair, wearing complementing Stetsons and even larger smiles, waved as they approached.

"Welcome to the Top Dog Dude Ranch," the woman called.

"We've been watching the weather that was blowing in on your route. Glad to see you made it safely." Jacob extended a hand to Riley.

"We're glad to be here." Lucy looked up at the Christmas lights hugging every corner, peak and window frame of the main lodge.

Her face was as bright as the lights, which, he reminded himself, was why she really needed this break too.

George wriggled to get down and then squished snow between his gloves. "Is it true that Santa is here?"

Hollie knelt. "You must be George. And yes. Santa is currently operating a train ride. Do you want to see him?"

"Yes, ma'am, please," he answered, leaning against his mom's leg as he did when feeling a little shy around someone new.

"Okay, folks," Jacob said. "If you head down this main road for about three minutes, then you'll see Santa's train station on your right. Y'all can walk and leave your car here. Your cabin should be ready after some holiday magic with Santa."

George's pile of snow fell to the ground. He jumped, giggling as he started down the road. Pure joy sounded in every crunch of snow beneath his boots.

This was the holiday spirit in action.

"Thank you. We will see you later," Riley called, rushing to keep up with George.

George's hurried pace made quick work of collapsing the distance to the train ride. A puppy just ahead of them tugged at the leash, stopping the handler short, which brought Riley up short so fast that Lucy bumped into him. His arm shot out to wrap around her shoulder, steadying her for a charged moment.

The older gentleman glanced back apologetically. "I'm so sorry. She's walked perfectly the whole week we've been here. I don't know what got into our sweet Daisy."

His wife tucked a hand into the crook of his

elbow. "Maybe Daisy's channeling some of that Top Dog magic to play matchmaker."

His arm went tense as silence stretched. Then Lucy burst into laughter, the sound wrapping around him until he joined in. As they walked through the still-fresh white snow, Lucy's cheeks flushed pale pink which made her green eyes seem even more bright and awake. He was glad to see his friend full of light and levity.

When was the last time she'd looked so enchanted?

An open-air trolley drew closer, whistle blowing. A puff of steam wafted up from the miniature stack at the front. The shiny blue engine was driven by Santa, with four covered cars behind. Each person loading up seemed to advertise happily-ever-after.

A family with three kids clambered into a train car.

A young couple sat in the caboose, his arm around her, her hand resting on her pregnant stomach.

A large crowd of what appeared to be a multi-generational family lined up to pile into three train cars. How surreal to see great-grandchildren. To have been married to the same person for decades. To see your life unfold in a way that wasn't full of heartache and mistakes.

Exiting the train area, a man with cropped salt-and-pepper hair laughed. His wife, a woman with silver-white hair and an easy smile resting on her lips, kept pace. The two paused, exchanging a knowing stare.

The older man patted Riley's arm while his wife cooed, "What a beautiful family you have."

Family? The assumption stung in a way that made him consider he was further from having a family now than he'd ever been. For the first time since he'd asked Lucy to join him on this trip, he wondered if he might have been better off sleeping on her sofa with Pickles.

Their log cabin was magical. Beyond imagining.

Tucked away in a notch in the forest, the little wood cottage had a covered front porch alight with white icicles. A towering pine out front was wrapped in multicolored lights. Through the trees they saw the distant twinkle of other cabins while still maintaining a peaceful retreat vibe, as if they were on their own in the woods.

Although the peaceful part could change when George woke up.

She climbed the steps, clutching the dog leash, Riley behind her holding an exhausted George. Once they'd finished the train ride and checked in, George had gobbled two granola bars, insisting that's all he would eat for supper, then promptly fallen asleep on the car trip to their cabin. So, they'd decided to put George to bed and have a late dinner in the cabin.

A wreath hung on the door with a wooden bone that read Santa Paws. She would have to take notes about the decor for ideas for her dog-walking business. She tapped in the security code and the door swung wide.

Warmth of all kinds flooded her senses. A crackling fire cast an orange glow over the hardwood floors. The cold of the afternoon fell away with the scent of pine and Douglas fir—no doubt the result of the decorated tree adjacent to the fireplace in the far end of the cabin. Off to the left, she noted a door, likely to the bedroom where she could tuck George in.

She slipped off her son's boots while he rested in Riley's arms, appreciating how easy Riley made things for her. Then, boots successfully removed, she reached for George and said softly, "I'll settle him for the night."

"He's heavy. I've got him. I'll just set him on his bed in his clothes and put a blanket over him. How about you order supper for us?"

"Can do." She smiled as he carried her son into the master bedroom.

Through the open door, she could see a small cot tucked in a sitting-area alcove. The quilt on his little bed was patterned with red doghouses and a blue cowboy hat waited on the pillow. Her heart warmed. George would be so excited to wear it when he woke up.

She dialed the number for the lodge kitchen and was put on hold, Christmas tunes playing over the line advising that orders could be placed online. She disconnected and waited for Riley, taking the opportunity to explore the open-concept downstairs.

A fat Christmas tree towered in the corner, decorated in tiny horseshoes and small ceramic dogs. Decorative wrapped boxes waited underneath. A plaid dog bed was tucked in the corner, food and water bowls beside waiting for Pickles to claim. Cast-iron pots and skillets hung on the walls in the kitchen. The chandelier looked like small lanterns.

The fireplace crackled with flames from gas logs and she curled up in a red plaid wing-back chair. Relaxing into the cushiony softness, she felt like she could sleep for days…or longer. But she should have dinner first, which meant placing the order. She clicked through and found the evening's menu with two options—either an appetizer platter or the brisket dinner. Easy enough to pick.

Hearing Riley return, she straightened in the wing-back. "I'll help you unload the car."

"No need," he insisted.

She stopped short at finding Riley standing with a basket of chocolates and champagne. "Oh my."

"This was in the bedroom." He shrugged in chagrin. "Jacob assured me he'd cleared away the whole honeymoon vibe, but I guess he overlooked a few things."

A twinge of regret pinched her as she thought of all Riley was missing in not having a real honeymoon. While she and Colin had more than their share of difficult memories, they'd also enjoyed a dream getaway to the beach, complete with days lounging in the sand, sipping umbrella drinks and planning for their future.

She shook off the past before it stole anything more from the present. "I ordered supper. It should be here soon. But the info in my binder says you have the deluxe granola snack package in the pantry if you're hungry now. A bit more substantial than champagne and chocolate, and it definitely beats the animal crackers and peanut butter sandwiches I packed."

"I can wait." He dropped into the other wing-back by the fireplace. "Remember how you used to pack double in your school lunches and then share with me?"

Firelight flickered, illuminating the hard lines of his jaw. The easy grace of his smile tugging his mouth upward at the memory.

"You were a growing boy."

And he'd sure grown in to a broad-chested hunk of a man. Under the camouflage of evening shadows, she allowed herself to indulge in a lingering perusal of her best friend—his strong thighs in well-worn jeans, his dark eyes warm with shared memories.

"I was a fourteen-year-old teenager with a bottomless pit for a stomach. Your mom had to wonder how in the world you were eating so much."

"She knew the truth. We didn't keep secrets. I miss her." It had been especially rough not having her around during the divorce. Not for the first time, she was so grateful for Riley.

"You had a good role model in the motherhood department."

"Thank you. I'm just not so sure I had much of an example from either of my parents on what it looked like to be in a healthy marriage."

Awkwardness cast a pall over the brief moment of…peace. Her relationship history had been shoddy at best. And she would do well to remember that. For herself. For her son. And yes, for Riley's sake, as well.

She shouldn't be trading long glances with her best friend now of all times, when he'd just suffered a devastating breakup. What was she thinking to let herself fall into the warmth of his brown eyes and imagine the strength of his strong arms?

She shot to her feet before she let herself get too comfortable with this setup. "While we wait for the food, let's get the rest of the luggage and then I can change into some pj's."

Very unattractive, flannel pj's.

Riley closed the door after the delivery man from the lodge, the dinner arriving just in time to keep him from having to untangle whatever had set Lucy on edge. Maybe she was just tired and hungry. No doubt when she missed meals she got "hangry."

The delivery man had placed their food on a rolling cart, each dish in a covered container. The soft sound of Lucy's footfalls drew his attention back to her. She looked too cute in her snowflake-patterned sleep pants and an overlong sweatshirt. Her fuzzy socks were mismatched—one pink and one green.

How could she appear so approachable and so very distant all at once?

"Dinner arrived." He motioned to the wooden tea cart.

"I can't believe we're really here," she said with an overbrightness to her tone that was all the more distancing for the fake quality. Lucy was normally anything but fake. "The view is stunning. You really did an amazing job researching."

"I have to confess—it's even better than I remember." He took his cue from her, moving the conversation back to the casual. "I drove over to check it out, but that was last fall. Everything was about harvest festivals and pumpkins. It's like a whole different place now."

"I saw something in one of the brochures about a spring vows-renewal extravaganza." Her eyes went a darker green, her fists tight.

He understood the feeling well…far better than he had in the past. "You and I are a jaded pair."

She pulled a smile, shaking her hands loose before walking to the old-fashioned tea cart full of covered dishes. "Let's just kick back and enjoy dinner. If it tastes even half as good as it smells, then it's amazing."

He gestured to the glassed-in porch with a snowy mountain view. Nodding, she pushed the tray through, stopping beside the quaint table.

Pulling out a chair for her, he waved for her to

sit. "This certainly beats the run-down place I took you to for our senior prom."

Her loose hair swept across his arm in a red flame as she took her seat, a whiff of her cinnamon scent drifting upward. "Oh my gosh, I haven't thought about that meal in forever. You meant well, though. It wasn't your fault the other place had a kitchen fire."

"And the best I could manage at the last minute on prom night was a drive-in burger joint."

"It was a great burger, though." She lifted the covers on the dishes to reveal smoked brisket, warm sweet-and-sour potato salad with flecks of bacon, crispy green beans and steaming cornbread with a dish of honey butter. And for dessert—pecan pie.

Memories of that night—and their kiss—flooded him, filling his senses with the remembered taste of her and the hint of caramel. Along with a sweetness that went beyond any dessert. Had the memory stayed as strong for her?

Averting her eyes, Lucy drizzled the honey butter over the cornbread. "Thank you for arranging those extra gifts for George to be waiting under the tree. You've really gone above and beyond."

"It was fun. I even managed to locate a toy garbage truck, as George requested."

"He will be so excited. Thank you." She spooned

a bourbon sweet barbeque sauce over her serving of brisket. "I can't even begin to pay you back for everything. If you get a dog, you will have unlimited dog-sitting and dog-walking services."

"Now that Emily's in the past, I can get a puppy. That's one bonus to the whole mess." He'd done his best to stay busy, putting those thoughts behind him whenever possible, but sitting here, still, it all came crashing back down on him. And it was all his own fault for choosing so badly. "Could have been worse, though. Better I found out now."

She touched his hand, her eyes filling with more of that sympathy that ate him up and made him all the angrier at Emily. Why couldn't he and Lucy have just come here like two friends without all the complicated baggage? How might the vacation have played out?

Lucy pulled her hand back. "Thank you for dinner. But if it's alright with you, I'd like to put the rest of mine in the fridge and go to bed."

Chapter Four

After a restless night, Lucy gave up and decided to soak in the cabin's copper bathtub. She sank deeper until the water lapped over her shoulders as she watched the sunrise through the circular stained glass window high in the wall. Pickles snored on the bath mat. The claw-footed tub took up most of the space but that seemed to just give the room more of a spa feel.

She didn't get many opportunities for a lazy morning, but George was still sleeping hard after the full day and she needed to use the time to get her head together. Flower petals floated around her, steam carrying the scent of roses.

Any other time, the perfume would have been soothing. But right now, with her thoughts so full of Riley, she couldn't help thinking of the rose corsage he'd given her when they went to senior prom together. She'd told him he didn't have to go to the trouble. They were just friends. She'd stopped shy of telling him not to spend the money since she knew how he paid all his own bills. He was prideful.

But Riley had insisted on the works—flowers and dinner before the dance. Her mind filled with memories of that night, of landing at the burger joint…

Lucy couldn't decide which smelled better, the rose corsage or the French fries.

Her lemon-yellow dress was covered in paper napkins to protect it from stray trails of the secret, savory sauce at Alfie's Dive Diner. Soft rock and roll played on the outside speakers at the drive-in burger restaurant. A carhop on roller skates zipped past.

Riley pointed with his burger in hand. "That guy over there in the Suburban full of children looks just like Abraham Lincoln."

Lucy laughed, awarding him the point in their game of celebrity look-alike. On the back of the re-

ceipt, she'd drawn two columns and kept careful tally. Riley was up by three points now. "That couple in the Mercedes coupe—" *They were dressed for prom too, no doubt also having lost a reservation at the same restaurant.* "Those look like the two teens from that movie we watched last weekend."

He thumbed the fraying leather on the sedan's steering wheel. "Sorry about the beater car."

"It runs. It's great. And so are these fries." *She popped another French fry into her mouth, savoring the salt on her tongue.*

"Dad had to, uh, work so I couldn't borrow his new truck tonight." *He avoided her eyes as he often did whenever the subject of his father came up.*

She knew his dad had a drinking problem—everybody knew—but he clammed up anytime anyone pressed for details.

"I mean it. It's really okay." *She didn't want to let anything spoil this evening.* "I'm just enjoying celebrating senior prom with you."

"You're being kind...and not just about the car." *He scratched along his neck, tugging at the collar of his tuxedo shirt.* "I found out you were supposed to go with a group of your friends for a girls' night out."

"You're my friend too." She touched his arm. "My best friend."

He understood her better than anyone else. With him, she never had to put on a social face or pretend. Being "real" was tough to do in high school.

"Well, Lucy, I'm glad, whatever the reason." He quirked a one-sided smile. "Although from the photos on social media, it looks like their dinner plans worked out better than ours."

"Riley, listen to me." She shifted in her seat, napkins sliding to the floorboards, and took him by the lapels. "Stop comparing. I'm where I want to be."

"Me too." He took one of her hands in his. "It's nice we're getting to spend this time together before I leave."

Frowning, she angled back to search his eyes in the dashboard lights. "Leave for where?"

"I landed a job at a ranch, starting right after graduation. I'll get to ride as often as I want without saving up to buy stable time. It's a dream come true for me."

"That's great news." She took his hand again, squeezing. "I'm happy for you. Where is it?"

"Up near Louisville."

She went cold inside, struggling to resist the urge to yank her hand back. "But that's nearly *three hours away." Same state, but so far. Why hadn't she heard of this plan before? "Is this because of what happened with your date tonight?"*

He snorted. "She wasn't that important. I've been looking for a job for a couple of months."

And he hadn't told her. That hurt. Really hurt. So much for friendship. She looked down, picking at the ribbon on her corsage, at a total loss for words.

"Hey," Riley said, tucking a knuckle under her chin. "I'll come back to see you. And you'll come to see me."

Lucy stared past him, focusing on the lights from a nearby Mustang convertible pulling out of the drive-up. "Sure."

"The spread is amazing. I'll be traveling with the owner's family to rodeos. I'm out of here, Lucy. I'm out." He paused. "Are you okay?"

No. She wasn't. Not at all.

And she didn't care about all the reasons she should be happy for him any more than the reasons she should hope he would make up with his girlfriend. Even though he hadn't told her about his plans, all she cared about right now was that she didn't want to let him go.

She threw her arms around his broad shoulders and hugged him to her. His shock must have been

*what made it so easy to move him. His gasp of sur-
prise was warm against her neck.*

*Then his hands slid up her back, one palm-
ing between her shoulder blades, the other lightly
touching the back of her neck in a way that made
her tingle. Melt.*

And that was before his mouth skimmed hers.

*She had no idea friendship could pack such
a powerful connection. She gripped his lapels,
clenching the fabric in tight fists. His low growl of
appreciation sending a thrill through her.*

*Then a tap on the window splashed a dose of
reality.*

*She flew back into her seat. The stunned ex-
pression on his face—no smile—doing little to reassure her. Especially since he was leaving in a
few short weeks.*

*Clearing her throat, Lucy pointed over his
shoulder. "Our milkshakes are here."*

"Milk, please!" George's voice drifted through
the bathroom door.

Past and present pressed together as the light
from the morning became brighter, filtering
through the honey and forest green stained glass.
Lucy plucked the drain plug, watching the petals
swirl down and away, along with her moment's

peace. That kiss had rocked her eighteen-year-old world. She knew that wasn't her imagination.

And she also knew she hadn't imagined his response—the attraction and the shutdown. She understood him too well, then and now. He'd been set on his path to leave and those plans didn't include more from her than friendship.

How frustrating for all of that to knock around inside her head at this particular moment, just because this time reminded her of then in a couple of superficial ways. This was totally different. They were different people.

Hauling herself from the tub, she reached for the plush towel hanging on a rustic ladder.

And sloshed water all over her clothes.

Riley almost tripped over his own feet when he saw Lucy sprint from the bathroom to the bedroom wrapped in only a towel, clutching dripping-wet clothes, Pickles following close on her heels. Seeing her slim legs and the sway of her hips sent his body into overdrive.

She nearly skidded into the bough of the white-lit tree, emerald-green towel catching briefly on one of the branches as Pickles barked. The scruffy dog wove between her legs, slowing her progress until she regained her balance.

Riley had seen his best friend hundreds of times in swimsuits over the long friendship. But he couldn't shake the spark that sizzled through him now. The same spark that had led him to kiss her when they were eighteen burned as bright as the star on the treetop.

"Sorry, sorry, my clothes got sloshed," she called out waving her hand just before slamming the door closed behind her, her voice drifting through. "I'll only be a minute. I really thought George would sleep a little longer. If you could just give him one of the milk boxes I put in the fridge."

"Sure," Riley pushed the single-syllable word out since he didn't trust his voice on much more.

Hearing her head into the bathroom earlier had broken into his dream as he'd slept on the sofa. Even after he'd stashed away his blankets and pillow, the muffled light splash of her in the tub had kept him very awake, his mind filling with images of her sinking into that claw-foot tub.

Seeing her in the towel now?

Whoa. Just whoa. What a massive distraction he did not need right now, so close on the heels of a breakup. He was a train wreck in the relationship department.

Eyes averted, he hauled his focus back on the present, welcoming the blast of cold air from the refrigerator. He pushed past the leftovers from their dinner and found the two little milk cartons. He pulled one out and popped in the straw. "George? Here's your milk, buddy."

George ran circles around the cabin, swooping by Riley to snag the carton with a "thank you" and three deep gulps before he resumed his zoomies. Pickles, who hadn't made it into the master suite before Lucy shut the door, wagged his tail before bounding after George. It was a wonder the boy's feet didn't slip out from under him in those footed holiday pj's.

"Careful that you don't fall with that."

"Okay, bein' careful." George stopped in front of the Christmas tree, drained his milk, then set it aside. He crawled around looking at presents.

Laughing, Riley bumped the refrigerator door closed. The kid's holiday spirit was infectious. The creak of the bedroom door drew his attention in a flash. Lucy rushed back in, pulling a long white sweater over her head, jean leggings hugging her slim legs. She made morning look good.

"George," she called, running past Riley, "those wrapped boxes are just for decoration, honey. Please don't shake them."

"But they're heavy." He pushed one out from under the tree. Wonder flicked over his face as he squinted at the perfectly wrapped present. "Heavy enough to be a garbage truck, maybe."

"It can't be, kiddo, because those aren't ours," she repeated. "Our gifts are the ones in the solid green paper and the solid red paper—"

"Uhm, Lucy," Riley interrupted, leaning close enough to catch the hint of roses perfume clinging to her skin. "These are the things I ordered ahead of time and had them wrapped to be ready and waiting."

Although the garbage truck would be delivered at a meeting with Santa.

"Oh, right. I'm so flustered." She sagged to lean against the back of the sofa, combing her finger through her damp red tendrils. "That was so sweet of you."

He clenched his fingers to ward off the phantom feel of moving her hands aside and untangling her hair himself. "It was easier than transporting stuff."

"Whatever you say." She looked from her son then back to him. "Thank you, my friend."

Friend.

That word hung between them, a tangible reminder that they weren't a couple. They never had been other than for one brief kiss back in high school. But why was that on his mind more now?

Was he deliberately thinking about it more since

Emily accused him of deeper feelings for Lucy? What had Emily seen that he missed? Because nothing—not a single thing—had happened sexually between them after that kiss.

She moistened her lips with the tip of her tongue, then backed away. "We'll need to hurry up and get you dressed if we want to make snow cones and play reindeer games."

Riley welcomed the excuse to bolt for his turn showering. He didn't even care if the hot water was all gone.

Thirty minutes later, all bundled up, they were walking through the ranch's little town square. Just the three of them. They'd given Pickles a quick run in the snow, then left him to nap in his bed with a new toy.

The O'Briens had built quite a showplace. Shops clustered around a towering, decorated tree and an ice-skating rink. The lodge took up a significant amount of real estate, with the dining hall angling off the side, a covered wagon beside it. A gift shop fashioned to resemble a Wild West country store. A clothing boutique. A bakery and ice-cream parlor that specialized in human treats as well as the doggy kind.

George rode on Riley's shoulders—the best way

to keep the kid from running off while they decided what to do.

Lucy pointed to the rink as a young couple swirled gracefully around a cone. "Now, *that* is something I can get behind."

"Then let's lace up some skates and you can teach me." He gestured to the far side of the rink with kids enjoying sled rides. "George could have fun over there. It's not far away and gauging by all the staff members, it's well supervised."

A border collie mix bolted past them, kicking up snow as the pup approached a family of five that slowly and cautiously made their way onto the ice.

The pup's enthusiasm dusted Lucy in an additional layer of snow, adding to the light flurry that fell from the sky. She let out a rich, easy laugh as Riley reached out, brushing the bigger pieces that clung to her chunky black knit scarf.

"Really? Are you sure you want to?" She looked up at him with inquisitive green eyes, snowflakes catching on her lashes.

"Of course. You can even laugh if I fall flat." Winking, he nodded toward a family, slipping, piling onto each other in a flurry of arms and legs.

"I can't imagine you falling. Your rodeo days showed off your impressive balance."

"I've taken a tumble or two in my time off crazy horses."

Her smile faded. "I remember."

"I always appreciated having you there."

She stopped in front of the kiddy sledding area, turning to face him, her full attention focused on him. "You always got me the best seats. But I would have come even if I'd had to sit way up in the nose-bleed section."

Leaving her behind had been the toughest thing he'd ever done. He'd thought he was doing the right thing for her, letting her move forward with her life. Instead, he'd been away during the time she'd needed him most. When she'd been busy falling for a man who didn't deserve her.

Another whisper of that high school kiss teased at the edges of his mind. Before he could stop himself, he stroked a thumb over her bottom lip, brushing aside snowflakes. Her pupils went wide.

The voices and music in the skating rink faded for a moment…

George wriggled, his boots thumping lightly against Riley's chest. "Look over there! It's Rudolph!"

Lucy was hungry.

And no amount of food seemed to satisfy her, although she'd certainly tried since that instant when Riley had touched her bottom lip. Just stroking away snowflakes.

Yeah, right.

Tapping her foot to the country Christmas carols piping over the sound system, she nibbled on the warm gingerbread while her son checked out a lamb in the living nativity petting zoo. She could chill for a moment and gather her thoughts since Riley was keeping close to the four-year-old while chatting with the ranch's owner Jacob. Something to do with the land Riley had purchased to start his horse breeding farm. She needed to remember that no matter what was going on with this resurgence of an old attraction between them, he would be moving soon.

Would he really be content with ranch life longterm? It felt like a great fit for him to work with horses full-time and it certainly seemed he'd always wanted it. Or was she deluding herself because she didn't want him to travel as much? For him to be more accessible even if he did live farther from her? The same way she didn't want him to leave town after high school?

She hoped she'd matured since then. She prayed that was the case. But how could she be sure? Not that it was a dilemma she could solve in the moment.

Better to focus on enjoying the present, which truly was so precious and perfect for George. The petting-zoo nativity had a donkey, lambs and even a camel.

A dark haired woman stepped up beside her, pausing. "Hello, I'm Hollie O'Brien," she said in a cheery voice, her name tag on the red reindeer scarf affirming her name and position as co-owner. "How are your accommodations? Are you enjoying your stay?"

"We are, thank you. It's a real treat to be able to offer an experience like this to my son." And to see him make those memories. His laughter floated on the winter wind as he moved from the sheep to a camel. She was glad his father wanted to spend time with him, but she wished she could see the smile on George's face as he enjoyed all those special things Colin had planned. Not that she could change that. She shook off the depressing thought. "Where did you get the camel?"

"It's on loan from the local zoo," Hollie said, her words riding a puff cloud into the cold air. "Just for a few days."

"Well, it's a big hit with George." Lucy soaked up the image of him posing on the camel for the camera. "The photos are going to be a priceless treasure."

Without even seeing the finished product, she already knew these captured moments would add to her collection of pictures on her mantel back home. And what photos of Riley might she be adding from this holiday?

"We are all about making memories here." Hollie pulled a pair of mittens from her pocket, tugged them on, then rubbed her hands together. "The photographer is from our other location. She's really a top-notch talent with a camera."

"I didn't realize you have another branch."

"It's not open yet, but it will be soon. We partnered up with a dairy farm outside Nashville."

"Nashville? That sounds like an amazing place to expand and how perfectly situated to tap into the country music scene."

"There will be more opportunities there for people who are looking for evening dates out on the town. We focus more on the retreat aspect here. Both bring together people with a love of nature." She pressed a hand over her heart, her dark hair stirring in the freezing wind. "Your son is quite the charmer. Be sure you take him to the reindeer rides."

"Real reindeer rides? Or like some kind of mechanical bull?" She plunged her glove covered hands into her coat pockets, feeling around for the itinerary.

"Actually, neither. Envision pony rides with little antlers on the harness."

"It sounds precious. Thank you for the pointer." How much did this woman know about Riley's situation with Emily? "And thank you for being so accommodating with the last-minute changes adding my son to the reservation."

"I'm glad we could work things out for Riley to still use the reservation. It's a great opportunity for him and Jacob to talk more about the land sale."

"Still, I'm sure you have a waiting list a mile long for people who could have taken the spot."

"We do. But we like to keep our customers happy. It's not the first time there's been a wedding cancellation."

Oh my. "What happened last time?"

"The groom gave the trip to his parents, then came here two years later with his new bride."

For a moment she thought Hollie was implying Lucy and Riley would become a couple down the road. Except the woman hadn't said anything of the sort. "I, uhm, hope Riley's heart mends that quickly."

"You never know what can happen when you

soak up the Top Dog magic." Hollie smiled, then backed away. "It's been nice chatting with you. Please don't hesitate to reach out if there's anything we can do for you."

Top Dog magic… Magic? Was that what this was all about? Some kind of fantasy, brought on by a well-crafted holiday venue and adorable animals?

She'd been drawn in by a fantasy vibe once before. She needed to keep reminding herself she wasn't a teenager anymore, in years or experience. It was time for her to start standing on her own two feet, beginning now. She pivoted on her heels to join her son and nearly tripped over a sheep she could have sworn wasn't there before.

"Lucy," Riley shouted from beside the camel. "Be careful of that patch of ice—"

His warning came an instant too late. The sheep let out a protracted "baaaaaa" just before another bump.

Lucy's feet shot out from under her and she landed smack on her bottom.

Chapter Five

With reflexes honed from years in the saddle, Riley shot across the snowy petting zoo toward Lucy, twenty yards away. Even knowing he wouldn't reach her in time didn't stop him from trying. Seeing her slip, topple over the sheep, then hit the ground sent a jolt of pain through him so intense he felt it in his teeth.

Concern for her sucker-punched him even harder.

"Jacob," he barked out quickly over his shoulder. "Please watch George."

Half registering Jacob's affirmation, Riley angled past a cow, another sheep and two kids in angel costumes. The crowd and holiday music faded in his mind, his focus narrowing to Lucy.

Only Lucy.

His boots gave him good traction on the icy patches. A hefty scattering of salt along the pathway helped him stay on his feet. Barrel racing had taught him to keep his eyes steady, focused on where he wanted to go. Needed to go.

But unlike on horseback, his legs could only move so fast. He lost sight of Lucy as a cluster of concerned people circled around her. His heart clenched in his chest.

"Excuse me," he said impatiently, clamping a hand on his Stetson to keep it anchored on his head. "Pardon me."

Finally, he made his way through the crowd to find her sitting on the ice, the sheep standing beside her looking too innocent for a creature that had moments earlier caused such mischief.

There didn't seem to be any blood. And Lucy had a chagrined smile on her face as she waved away help from others. He dragged in a grateful breath.

"Lucy, are you alright?" He knelt beside her, edging around the others. Thank goodness no one argued, because he wasn't looking for a fight. "Don't try to stand up yet. Are you nauseated?"

"No, I'm fine. Really."

He continued with concussion-protocol questions anyway since any hard fall could jolt the head. During his rodeo days, he'd seen people get their bell rung too often to take this lightly. Her speech wasn't slurred, her pupils were equal and she didn't seem dizzy.

"Can you tell how many fingers I'm holding up?"

"I'm fine." She braced a hand on his arm. "And you're holding up three. I *can* see, but I would also know that because you always hold up three fingers."

He would have laughed. An image of a fifteen-year-old, hay-tossed Lucy who'd fallen off the second rung of the barn ladder danced in his mind. In that fall, she'd busted her wrist and had to wear a cast for the entire summer. A fraction of a second in the past before catapulting back to the present. Another time where her internal sense of balance bested her.

He dragged in a steadying breath, somewhat reassured, but he would still be keeping a close eye on her. "I'll be sure to vary the number of fingers I hold up the next time someone decides to breakdance on the ice."

"Good to know. Now help me up, will you?" she asked, her teeth chattering.

"What if you're in shock?" Possible, but she was steady and she wasn't pale. "You might be numb. Give yourself a couple more minutes." And he needed that time too so his heart rate could return to something close to normal.

"If I sit here for two more minutes, I *will* be numb." Shivering, she tucked her hands into his. "Thanks, I'm good now. Let's collect George."

Her fingers squeezed around his ever so slightly, but enough that he gripped in return before he could stop himself. He looked into her eyes, the green deepening. Somehow just this simple touch, the way she looked at him in a way he knew he was one-hundred-percent seen.

And drawn to her.

His pulse cranked right up again.

A pack of teens walking a goat and a couple of sheep stopped, laughing as the goat head butted Riley in the back. Center of balance temporarily suspended, pressing him closer to Lucy's warmth.

Her green eyes went hazy hazel with emotion, wilder and more inviting than any Tennessee twilight sky. The connection wrapped around him. Steadied him for a moment as the space between them shrank. Breath caught in the air, swirling in the ever-smaller space between their heads. Their lips.

The tallest boy pointed, gathering the goat's lead. "Get a room, you two."

Lucy twitched, then stepped back. Riley quirked a half smile, all too aware that they already had a room. One they wouldn't be using for anything close to what those teens were thinking.

Lucy hadn't played dress-up since elementary school. But as she tied the bow on her bonnet for caroling, she had to admit—it was a welcome escape from thinking about how a "family" vacation with Riley may not have been the best idea. She swept a hand down the calico gown that looked like something out of a Wild West movie, complete with petticoats that provided so much padding it would have been a welcome addition when she'd fallen on her bottom earlier.

Heat tingled along her skin, more from embarrassment than the flames licking in the bedroom fireplace.

With a bracing breath, she scooped up the navy cape and matching mittens on her way to the living area. Her pointy black boots tapped along the wooden floor, then quieted on a braid rug.

Riley knelt by the hearth adjusting the ear flaps

on George's brown hat, then draped a plaid scarf around her son's neck. His care with her child touched her heart, as it always did.

But right now, she wasn't watching George. Her gaze was all about Riley, taking in every fantasy-worthy inch of him as he stood. It seemed that time went into slow motion, which she knew wasn't possible, but she savored all the same.

He wore an old-fashioned, umber leather duster with a vibe of Christmas cowboy meets steampunk that accentuated his already incredible shoulders. And tall… Lordy, he was tall and he hadn't even dropped his Stetson onto his head yet. Then he tipped his face toward her, his deep brown gaze colliding with hers. He looked her up and down in a way that was new, intimate. Because he'd seen her dash past in nothing but a towel earlier?

Or was it something else? Like that moment that had felt like an almost kiss after she'd fallen? She'd been so caught up in his touch, his concern, that she'd felt mesmerized by the warmth in his dark eyes.

A tap on the front door broke the moment and she sprinted across to answer. She clipped a leash on Pickles and swung the door wide. The sound of "Jingle Bells" swelled through the cottage, the merry tune riding a gust of cold air. A flock of other guests dressed up in old fashioned holiday finery lifted up their voices in song, accompanied by musicians playing a banjo, guitar and fiddle.

Winter scents of pine and snow filtered over through the threshold. Light glowed from the battery-operated candle lanterns held by the assembled group.

George yanked on the sleeves of his long jacket, flapping his arms like a bird. He cast her a glance that made her momma-bear heart swell. Wonder lit his cheeks that were already turning pink from the night air.

Magic, the kind that only belonged to the sound of community music, brought his hands together in excited, gleeful claps. Already it was turning into a perfect evening, seeing that look on her son's face, reminding her how grateful she should be to Riley for giving her this chance to make really special holiday memories with her child.

Bootfalls echoed behind her, then fell silent as Riley's familiar hand brushed against her back. A pose they'd probably adopted dozens of times over the course of their friendship.

Tonight though, the touch against her deep blue cape, his hand pressed to the small of her back, made her cheeks flood with heat. A charge snapped between them even as George shouted the third-to-last verse of "Jingle Bells." She kept her eyes averted, afraid of giving herself away. They knew each other too well, able to read emotions that weren't hidden well away.

Just ahead of them, another family stepped out of their cottage, looking more like something from Dickens's *A Christmas Carol*. The father wore a British top hat, long scarf, and carried a walking stick. His wife clutched a little silk purse while their daughter kept her hands warm tucked inside a fluffy white muff.

The whole caroling experience was a mash-up of costumes and time periods that came together in a masterpiece of holiday cheer. She sneaked a sidelong glance at Riley through her lashes, only to be blindsided again by how roguish he looked in his Wild West cowboy gear.

George took the first step from cabin to snow-crested ground while Riley shot out the door second. Her oldest friend in the world corralled her wild-child son. Laughter and wide smiles were rippling on a few of the carolers' faces as the last few lines of the song swelled in volume.

She scooped up Pickles, who was looking so unbelievably cute in a sweater with booties. He probably didn't need the clothes, but better safe than sorry with the cold weather and snow. They merged into the strolling merrymakers just as they launched into "Twelve Days of Christmas."

Lucy surrendered to the mood and hooked arms with Riley, determined not to let the untimely awareness between them diminish the holiday spirit of a fun night. What could possibly happen in these layers of clothes, outside, in a crowd?

Crunching steps into the snow, she took care to avoid ice—desperately wanting to channel the grace into her movements to avoid another ego-crushing slip and disrupt this fairytale setting. Lucy wished to keep this night forever unfolding. "This whole place has such a timeless quality."

"If only it were that easy to freeze the clock instead of our—"

She cleared her throat and nodded toward George making friends with another boy about his age dressed up in a dark cape with a lace collar from another century, a wool newsboy cap on his head. "I'll settle for savoring the now. I love the attention to detail. It's a winter wonderland and holiday retreat all rolled into one, without being hokey."

"You have a great eye for the particulars. What things would you add?" Riley's warm brown eyes flicked from her back to George and his new friend as they stopped in front of the next squat cabin with a chimney working overtime, sending plumes of gray smoke into the violet twilight.

"I'll have to mull that over."

They hung slightly back from the active carolers, the tune transitioning from the "Twelve Days of Christmas" to "Jingle Bell Rock." A staff member wove through the crowd, distributing jingle bells to eager children which included George and his new friend.

Taking in the sight and a big lick from Pickles, she smiled, arriving at the only missing detail. "Bells on the dog leashes so everywhere we go it sounds like sleigh chimes."

At the chorus, George and his new friend jumped, shaking their bells at each other. "I like that. I'll have to add that to my list for next year on my horse farm." He glanced at her. "Or you and George could come spend next Christmas with me. Bring Pickles. We'll reenact all of our favorite parts about this place there."

His talk about future holidays sounded an awful lot like building a family tradition. In the past, she wouldn't have given a second thought to such a notion, but as their friendship entered new terrain? This felt…different. Could there be a future where her best friend would be her family too? Would that be okay?

Her gaze skipped to the others, so many relatives celebrating together. The family in the cabin gave a round of applause as the group turned back to the path, making their way toward the main lodge. Vanishing sunlight silhouetted the lodge, making their final destination seem enchanted against the indigo sky.

"Are you going to dress up as Santa next year with the sleigh?"

"Are you into dress-up?"

Her eyebrows shot up. He couldn't have meant that in a risqué manner. Or had he? "Uhm, well, I…"

Chuckling, he slid an arm around her shoulders. "You can pretend I didn't say that. It must have been a Freudian slip."

So his mind was "going there" too. This wasn't her imagination. Heat stung her cheeks.

And fantasies filled her mind of him in that duster, her in a saloon-girl costume…

She forced those thoughts to scatter, appreciating that he wasn't making her feel awkward over a whoops of an innuendo. "It's been surreal pretending everything's okay, that nothing's changed. But maybe that's better. I say we keep right on with that, because heaven knows we could both use some fun for the holidays."

"Alright then. Challenge accepted."

Wow, he'd sure agreed to that awful fast. Too fast. Disappointment stung more than it should.

As the group walked toward the lodge, the children had all banded together in the front, George radiating excitement to have kids his age to sing with. Echoes of "Ho-ho-ho" filled the air as the staff now played "Up on the Housetop."

His forehead furrowed. "You believe me, don't you? If I say I'll honor your request, I mean it."

"Of course, I believe you." She hugged Riley's arm tighter to her side. "If we can't trust each other, then who can we ever believe?"

The words resonated, perhaps even a bit too much.

"You have a point." There was no missing the seriousness in his response. But as quickly as it arrived, he shifted back to the lighthearted tone that had been signature to their relationship for over a decade. "I can't imagine trusting anyone else to choose a tattoo for me."

"That worked both ways."

After graduation, before he left, they agreed to get tattoos, each choosing what the other would get and it would be a surprise after. They would both look at the same time.

For her, he'd chosen two paw prints. For him,

she'd chosen two horseshoes. And how ironic that they'd selected tattoos for each other that were in many ways the same...same size, a pair.

At the time, they hadn't considered what it would mean to explain that inking to somebody else. Colin had said he didn't care, that he wasn't threatened by the friendship. But her marriage certainly hadn't been the gold standard when it came to healthy relationships. Which also made her wary of trusting her judgment a second time.

So where did that leave her? With a broken marriage, a tattoo and a sexless future.

Snippets of the next song became wind-caught now that she and Riley had lagged farther behind, but still close enough to see and hear her son with his new little friends. Her ears filled with the roaring lilt of "Auld Lang Syne." Whispers of her past tugged at her now, mixing with the words the carolers sang as they made their way to the second-to-last cabin on the path. The song made her feel sentimental about old friends.

Made her want to celebrate a friendship that had been the bedrock for her.

She didn't understand the wayward feelings she'd been having toward Riley this week, but she knew she appreciated him in her life and George's.

She stepped in front and turned to face him, arching up on her toes…

And she kissed him.

Just a quick press of her lips against his. Sensation shimmered through her veins that made her ache to lean in for more. Then his hand palmed her back, that warm press reminding her they were in a crowd of people.

More important, they were only a few feet away from George with the other kids and she couldn't afford for him to misunderstand.

Angling back from Riley, she plastered a smile on her face and said, "Merry Christmas. Let's join the others and sing."

By the next afternoon, Riley didn't have any more clue than the day before as to what Lucy was thinking. Which was a strange feeling. In a world full of uncertainty, they'd always been able to count on transparency with each other.

Right now, Lucy was the opposite of transparent.

She'd avoided him like crazy. During lunch, she'd decided to rearrange decorations on the tree, waving away his question with the excuse that she just couldn't sit. Afterward, she'd tucked into a chair with her phone to place an online grocery order, turning aside his offer to take her out to lunch.

He watched her, his fingers steepled under his chin as she stood at the kitchen counter unloading the bag of groceries she'd had delivered. Red hair rippled like gentle waves down her back as she reached into the sturdy paper bag—something about making George's favorite peppermint chocolate bark. Even though they had a whole pantry full of food and treats, plus an entire restaurant and bakery at their disposal. She was a flurry of movement.

Avoiding him.

She'd kept to herself since bailing on that brief kiss in the moonlight. She'd barely said two words to him during the festivities with Santa in the main lodge, instead making small talk with another young mother while George had his photo taken with jolly ole Saint Nick.

Wasn't that why he'd invited her and George to come along? To make happy holiday memories to wipe out the bad? It wasn't as if they were an actual couple.

Sure, he found her attractive. She was an undeniably beautiful, sexy woman, with a big heart and quick wit. But he knew the kiss was just an impulse, like in high school. And he was tired of being shut out of what was on her mind.

The way she was ignoring him now, though, gave this kiss a weight that went beyond that one in high school.

Reliving that simple encounter while they were caroling… Yeah, he felt the connection, even if he hadn't acted on it. It was a simple kiss that was probably his fault anyway for making that silly crack about playing dress-up.

And his mind definitely didn't need to go there. Not now. Not ever.

At least he had a moment to shield his face so she wouldn't catch a hint of his thoughts either.

Her back to him, she placed a double boiler on the gas stove. "You don't have to stay in here with me." She sighed hard, calling his attention to the curves that pushed against her dusty-pink sweater. "I've got plenty to keep me occupied while George sleeps."

He was done being ignored. He shoved to his feet and joined her at the counter, then leaned against the butcher block so he could face her. "Are you firing me as your sous chef already?"

She opened a cabinet and pulled out measuring cups, adding them to the neat row of her ingredients. White chocolate. Peppermint extract.

A package of bright red-white-and-green candy canes. Coconut oil. Dark chocolate. For as long as he could remember, Lucy always arranged her baking ingredients on the counter in the order they'd be needed.

"I think you deserve to enjoy this trip you paid for." Lucy's smile seemed infused with the same brisk wilderness that unfurled out the window in the drifting snow. Not uninviting, but hesitant. "I'm sure you didn't originally sign on for the kiddie package."

Was that what the cold shoulder was about? Her worrying that she was in the way? Ridiculous. "How about this? If there's something else I want to do, I promise to let you know."

"I'm going to hold you to that."

"Good." He lifted the peppermint extract and inhaled the scent. His mouth watered, his senses kicking memories into overdrive. Maybe that was the key to getting through to her. "I can still taste those peppermint brownies your mom used to make every December."

"I've tried to replicate them. And tried. I got tired of wasting money on the ingredients only to throw them in the trash." Her words picked up speed, the memory doing its trick in getting her to open up. "So now I opt for the peppermint bark, which seems to fit the theme of my dog-dominated world better."

He fiddled with the coconut-oil bottle, thumbing the lid so it made a gentle popping sound as golden rays from the still-crisp day filtered through the thick glass panes.

"In those days I was so hungry to be a part of a real family, I probably would have eaten cardboard and thought it was a delicacy if it meant spending more time in your mom's kitchen."

Back then, he and Lucy had enjoyed hours at the island in the center of the bright white farmhouse-styled kitchen. They would do their homework there, talk about their plans, while her mother whipped up snacks she'd called *brain fuel*—hummus and veggies, cheese and crackers. Things that were tough to come by at his house.

Lucy and her mom hadn't been wealthy, but there were always touches in the space that made it feel rich in ways that mattered. Vanilla-and-lemon-scented candles lit by the large window that overlooked the tiny, but well-tended, backyard. Baby's breath flowers in an old glass milk jug and bits of stacked mail.

"Mom liked you."

"Your dad didn't."

Her face relaxed and she laughed softly. "Dad doesn't like anyone."

"That's not exactly true. He adored you."

Her smile faded. "That made my parents' divorce all the harder, seeing two people I loved, who loved me back, hate each other so bitterly."

Seeing her gaze skate to the bedroom where George napped with Pickles reminded him again how complicated relationships would always be for her, given the baggage from her parents' breakup. Then her own. She deserved better from all of them—from him too. He would do anything to shield her from further heartbreak, protect her from anyone who could leave another scar on her heart.

Including himself.

He set the coconut oil onto the counter with a light thud. "You know, I think you're right. I should go check out the stables while I have the chance."

Chapter Six

This vacation grew more complicated by the day.

Rather than a laid-back, easy getaway with her best friend, every event with Riley left her feeling tense and confused. Even something as simple as Christmas baking—which she'd hoped would help her restore equilibrium after that impulsive kiss—had instead led to a conversation fraught with land mines from her childhood.

Since Riley had left her standing in the kitchen with a counter filled with the makings of peppermint bark a couple of days ago, they'd spent more and more time doing individual events. She was glad George was having a blast, truly, and she loved her son.

So why did she feel the holiday spirit was lacking its usual glitter for her? Like she was going through the motions for her child?

Leaving lunch, she squeezed George's gloved hand clutched in hers. "Did you have fun with the gingerbread-man piñata?"

He clutched his doggie bag of candy and tiny toys to his chest. Snow gathered on his dark blue jacket, his boots crunching ice as he walked. "It was so fun. Can you believe I knocked off one of the legs?"

The adults had even been given the opportunity to smack out some frustration by pounding the gingerbread-man piñata a couple of times. Since Riley hadn't come, she'd spent the party talking with the young mother of the boy George had partnered with to build a snowman.

As two young moms, they'd bonded over shared tales of relationship woes. In fact, most everyone here seemed to be working on healing a relationship—which didn't do much to help her question her own trust issues.

"I saw. You were a rock star, kiddo." She slid an arm around his shoulders and hugged him closer. "I'm so glad you're my little boy. I love you."

"Love you, too, Mommy," he said before fishing around in his treat bag and pulling out a little candy cane. He held it up with a smile. "Here ya go."

"Thank you. You're so sweet to share even when Santa isn't watching."

His giggle carried on the wind and then was cut short. "Look over there." He pointed toward the parking lot, fuller than normal with vehicles and people. "It's Riley."

Riley?

She searched the crowd gathered around a half-dozen pickup trucks being loaded—with wire kennels, dog beds, boxes labeled as dog toys. Even a local news station had a van parked nearby.

Wind billowed, stirring the ombré hair of a nearby teen dressed in a thick, puffy coat with the Top Dog Dude Ranch logo. Other employees wearing elf hats and their staff jackets chatted while loading dog food, their breaths and conversations crystalizing in the air.

Horses milled around near the split rail fence, taking it all in while being fed carrots by a cluster of children.

Brave young souls.

Sure, she knew they were safe and supervised. But still, horses, especially large ones, scared her silly.

Her gaze then landed on Riley, and her stomach

did a little flip. Even from the back, she would recognize those broad shoulders anywhere. He hefted up a massive bag of dog food then slung it onto a pile in the back of one of the pickups. Over and over again, tirelessly.

George arched up onto his toes. "What's that?"

An older couple in bright orange jackets pulled up beside them, their names and the Top Dog logo stitched on the nylon—Patsy and Lonnie.

Chilly breeze lifting his whispery salt-and-pepper hair, Lonnie offered George a crinkly smile. "Well, young man, every year at Christmas we take up donations for a local animal shelter. People in the community donate, but we also get contributions from individuals who've stayed here in the past. The outpouring is really incredible, the true spirit of Christmas."

He clapped his hand to his chest, good cheer flushing his cheeks that had already begun to turn rosy from the cold.

"How wonderful," Lucy sighed, looking at the tables and waves of moving people.

Snippets of conversation mingled with the pine scent. And although she was doing her best to stay focused—stay present and here—Lucy's eyes wandered back to Riley dressed in his fleece-lined jacket, work-worn boots and Stetson. Stray snowflakes fell from the sky as he hefted another bag of dog food up on his shoulders. The effortless motion made her breath hitch for a moment.

Patsy pointed to a tent set up with a table, two adults leading kids in some kind of activity. "If you're interested, we also have a craft table over there for the children. The kids make cards for local health care employees who will be working over the holidays."

Lucy's gaze caught on the glitter as a young girl held up her card for inspection. "You seem to have thought of everything when it comes to helping people focus in on what really matters."

"We here at the Top Dog Dude Ranch sure do try," Patsy answered, holding out a hand for George.

He looked back at Lucy and she gave him an encouraging nod. He passed her his candy then raced over to the craft table, tugging off his mittens.

The children gathered under a tent making cards, surrounded by portable heaters. A border collie walked around with a basket in his mouth, the basket full of stickers for the children.

Patsy pointed to a boy and girl at the far end of the table. "Those are our grandchildren. We're so excited to have them here for the holidays."

Lonnie's bright eyes danced, catching a blue

flame from the sunlight as he spoke. "One year at Christmastime, we took the grandkids to Dollywood. Little Alexa got sick from riding the Lightning Rod. Her brother Andre teased her about that for years. Even made a song about it to taunt her when her friends came over."

Grinning, Patsy gave an exaggerated wink. "He gets his love of music from my side of the family. I was named for the great Patsy Cline."

Lonnie looped an arm around his wife's shoulders. "Now don't forget that we work here. Patsy and I are both certified massage therapists. We also teach classes in dog massage techniques to calm your pup, if needed."

"We mix the essential oils, as well." Patsy leaned into her husband's arm with a familiarity and ease that spoke of happy years. "The doggies especially love it when I rub just a bit of lavender oil on their ears."

Lonnie's eyes lit with mischief. "I love it when she dabs some lavender oil on my ears too."

Laughing, Patsy swatted his arm. "You're such a naughty boy. Watch out or Santa's gonna fly right past our cabin."

Their glances, the way they leaned in to each other with such gentle familiarity, defrosted some of the pain in her heart. Seeing this couple, the life they had built made her chest tighten, her heart ache. A whisper of a dream floated through her mind… They were clearly friends as well as lovers.

"If you're interested in essential oils, you may want to earmark our session tomorrow."

Lucy asked, "Is this one for the dogs?"

"You can bring your pup, of course, but this is about relieving stress for people." Patsy gestured with her hands, breathing in, breathing out. "Ways to ground yourself through the senses, in particular through the sense of touch and the sense of smell. We offer an assortment of oils that are holiday themed."

"We call it the Twelve Smells of Christmas— ginger, chocolate, pine, berries, cinnamon, cider, vanilla, pumpkin, eucalyptus, firewood and fresh snow." She paused for effect. "And peppermint."

Lucy's gaze gravitated right back to Riley, her stomach plummeting as she thought of their strained conversation earlier in the kitchen. For years, peppermint sweet treats bonded them together through everything—holidays and even regular Tuesdays too. Now a gulf seemed to exist between her and Riley. She couldn't shake the image of him leaving her in the kitchen, the way his jaw had flexed with frustration on his way out the door.

Patsy sighed, her neck craning to look at a young girl in pigtails who waggled her finger at a boy who shared her same upturned nose. She nudged Lonnie, calling her husband's attention to the scene. "It looks like Alexis is picking on her brother again. We should intervene before someone needs stitches."

Waving as they left, Lonnie and Patsy trailed off, keeping in step with each other as they picked their way closer to their grans.

Lucy tucked a stray piece of hair behind her ear, casting a quick glance toward Riley, then toward George. Her son's bright red curls played peaka-boo from beneath his beanie. Even from here, she could see his scrunched thinking face as he looked between two different colored markers.

"Lucy?"

Hearing her name, she turned toward two women in fluffy Top Dog Dude Ranch parkas and welcoming smiles. After a second look, she recognized the dark-haired ranch owner—Hollie—with the blonde lady who'd taken photos during the holiday petting zoo. Nina?

Lucy squinted into the afternoon sun, trying to read the name in black stitching on the pink parka. Yes, definitely Nina.

Nina paused, camera in hand as snowflakes

caught in her ash-blond hair and deep pink beanie, and called out to Lucy. "Would you mind being in a photo with Hollie?"

"Oh, uh," Lucy stuffed her cold hands in her pockets and backed away. "If you need me to move—"

"Not at all. You two just chat as if I'm not here. I may take some other pictures too. The angle here is fabulous."

Two steps forward, and Lucy was within comfortable distance from Hollie while still able to keep George in view. Lucy did her best to ignore the camera and stand naturally, as if she and Hollie were engaged in deep conversation. It was good not to feel at loose ends, awkwardly alone.

The goodwill of the day wrapped around her like a cozy blanket, all the sweeter for the surprise of its generosity at a time she was so confused on the inside. "I think this has been my favorite day of all."

"It feels good to give back." Hollie nodded, wind billowing her hair across her face.

"You've created an environment here that brings out the best in people." Lucy drew in a bracing breath of cold air—lungs stinging in a way that felt anchored. Alive and yet anxious, all at once, struggling to figure out what was going on with Riley.

As much as she tried to stop, her gaze kept moving back to him, trying to pinpoint what made him walk out of the kitchen at the time he did. What made him keep to himself since then? Had she somehow given off a sense of pushing him away and that was what he was reacting to?

"I can't take the credit for this place," Hollie dismissed the praise. "It's the animals. They bring all the magic for us. Some of our animals even came from that very shelter."

"Really?" she asked, curious. "Which ones?"

Hollie pointed toward the fence line at the pair of bay Tennessee Walking Horses. "Two of our horses were confiscated by the shelter from a neglectful owner. We rehabilitated them and then we were able to adopt them for our ranch."

"That's beautiful." Second chances were such a gift.

"There were three horses pulled—one didn't make it." Hollie glanced away for a moment, her throat moving in a slow swallow. "We named the next foal born here after that horse." The woman's eyes dimmed, her face tightening as her smile wobbled ever so slightly.

"Hollie, what a meaningful tribute to pass along

those names." Loss never got easier. Especially when that loss was tied to innocence. And while she knew the owner absented some of the contours of the story, Lucy was no stranger to the tapestry of loss. Pulling on one thread inevitably yanked and strained some other area of life.

There'd been a time she'd even pulled away from Riley when her mother died. She wondered how she hadn't healed better? Hadn't her mother's love taught her to open her heart more than that?

Drumming footfalls cracked the somber moment as George ran toward her. His face all upward angles of hope and smiles. "Mommy, Mommy, look at the two cards I made. They're for doctors and nurses who take care of little kids."

She sifted through each sweet tribute, thick cardstock paper bending slightly in her grip. "Wow, what a great job. I love the way you drew Pickles in his booties on this one. And a Christmas tree in front of a mountain on this one. I'm so proud of you."

She pulled him in tight for a hug. He wrapped his arms around her neck, the sweet-little-boy smell of him warming her heart. Then he wriggled free.

He reached into his coat and pulled out another card. "And look at this one I made for Daddy when I go see him."

* * *

Time was running out to enjoy this trip with Lucy and George to the Top Dog Dude Ranch. Riley needed to make the most of this afternoon at Santa's workshop, where children made crafts for gifts. He couldn't dodge the sense of time ticking down like before heading out of the chute into the ring.

Except Lucy was the one who would get hurt. Tomorrow was Christmas Eve. The day Colin would pick up George. And how did the kid feel about it? So far, Lucy seemed to be doing a wonderful—beyond fair—job at preparing him.

Yet, each word did little to decrease his own tension, all too aware of how badly holidays could turn out, thanks to his own father. How badly he'd jacked up relationship after relationship, and was in danger of wrecking his friendship with Lucy.

Maybe this ranch had something to teach him after all. Spending time here was showing him that maybe Emily had a point. He might lack the skills to enjoy a sense of family in the future if he couldn't even steer this visit with his best friend in a happy direction.

Riley returned his attention to the trio of elves teaching the crafting class for homemade gifts. At the center of the room, the leader elf leaned against the pine workbench that was set up to mirror the stations for the gathered group. He lifted his hands, drawing the attention of the room with a simple gesture.

Clearing his throat and adjusting his dark green Santa hat, the leader elf spoke with a lilt. "So many times, the best gifts we receive are the ones that people make for us. With that in mind, I'm going to lead you as you make treasures to share with people you love to remember this trip by."

Riley stole a glance at where Lucy stood with her arms crossed over her chest. Even from a distance, he could see the set of her jaw meant she was chewing on the inside of her lip. Her body was tense beneath her plum sweater with large fuchsia polka dots.

And more important, why was he noticing what she wore—noticing *her*—more and more these days?

What kind of memories would he make if he didn't get his head together? He reminded himself to be in the moment. There was still an awkwardness between him and Lucy, but he'd brought her and George here for a reason—to make *happy* memories.

George looked so cute standing on the footstool at the craft table with a tiny tool box for supplies, his name painted on the side. All the children had one, decorated with a globe beside their name in keeping with this workshop's theme of gifts from around the world.

Stations were set up throughout the space. There were wood crafts to paint—Russian nesting dolls, a wooden dreidel, Las Posadas lanterns, a kinara with candles.

A cloth-goods section included stamping squares of fabric with symbols to make an adinkra cloth, sewing pouches and filling them to make potpourri sachets. Holiday scents saturated the air.

Lucy leaned toward her son, red hair falling on the top of the curve of her breasts. "I'll be right back. I'm going to talk to the lady who took your picture earlier in the week at the petting zoo and the fund-raiser. I won't be too far away. She's right over there with her twin girls making nesting dolls."

George looked up from stamping dog paws on fabric sections. "Okey doke. Love you, Mom. Take your time."

He sounded like such a little old man sometimes.

Lucy wrapped him in a quick hug, dropping a kiss on his head before weaving around tables. Riley allowed himself the moment to just watch her walk, the sway of her hips, her efficient steps making her hair swish. His fingers ached to touch her, to see if she somehow felt different since she looked different to him these days in a way he'd yet to define. Although he'd done little else but try to sift through those feelings since he'd walked out of the kitchen.

Desire pooled in his gut, threatening his focus. He tore his gaze away from her before he did something ridiculous, like haul her under the mistletoe and kiss her senseless.

He stared out the window, sunlight bathing the fresh snow in a light glow. A buckskin quarter horse and a piebald horse trailed calmly behind a ranch hand. The pair was completely tacked as the ranch hand approached eager riders near mounting blocks.

How he wanted and needed to get in the saddle. To clear his mind and settle his soul. Maybe figure a way through this vacation that eliminated the distance between him and Lucy.

George craned his head to watch his mom walk away, then looked back at Riley quickly. "Hurry. I want to finish making this blanket for my mom."

He pulled his attention off the horses. "That's great, kiddo. But I think she may get back before we're done."

His little face fell with disappointment.

Riley cupped a hand on his small shoulder.

"How about I text her and ask to run some errands for us so we have more time to work?"

"Yeah," he said, nodding. "That's good. Thanks. You're the best."

Riley tapped his phone and swiped up his lock screen—a picture of Pickles, George and his mare Molly from two summers ago. For a moment, he paused on that image, reliving the sunshine and the way Lucy had been wringing her hands together as her baby boy approached his champagne mare.

Riley tapped away. Could you bring an extra sweater for George? He told me that he was too chilly to walk back later.

"Okay, kiddo, when your mom comes back and brings you an extra sweater give her a big thanks."

"Gotcha." George laid his supplies out with the same precision and desire for order Lucy had when baking. Smoothing the light tan cloth squares, George looked through the box of fabric stamps which held adinkra symbols for hope, peace, unity, strength.

"Your mom is going to be really excited when she opens this."

George picked up a stamp that featured a slice of moon and with a star overhead. "I like this one. What does it mean?"

Riley consulted the guide in the box. "Love and harmony."

George nodded solemnly. "It's perfect for Mommy."

With the utmost sincerity, George lined the symbol up with the center of the tan square of cloth and pressed hard. His face scrunched into a mask of intense concentration.

Riley fished a rendering of a heart which the guide said meant *take heart and use patience*. Fitting for where they were.

Satisfied with his first press, George looked into the box, studying his other options. Toying with the stamp in his hand, George bopped his head along to the *Nutcracker Suite* that played softly in the background.

The boy sighed as if liberating himself of a big secret as he pressed another symbol into the cloth. "Victor's my new friend. He told me not to be scared when a barrel fell off a truck and made a loud noise."

"I'm sorry you were frightened. Loud noises startle me every now and again too."

"He said his dog is afraid of lightning. I told him that sometimes Pickles barks when people ring the doorbell. But he said his dog hides under the bed and he crawls under there too to keep him company."

Riley wondered where George was going with this story, but he'd learned if he kept listening, affirming and giving the kid time to find the words, there was a message buried underneath waiting to be found. "Your new buddy sounds like he's a good friend to his dog."

"Yep." He smoothed out a new square of cloth. "Can I take Pickles to my daddy's house? I wouldn't want Pickles to get scared without me."

George chewed his lip, fear clouding in his brilliant blue eyes. Another habit Riley understood from his time with Lucy. The gesture came up when George was nervous, and it only stood to reason the kid was anxious about being away from his mom.

"You can ask your mom, but I'm pretty sure Pickles will be staying with us. But I'll tell you what. I will be very careful to make sure Pickles is okay. And your father has a dog too, remember? Maybe you could help that pup if she or he gets scared."

George mulled it over, then nodded. "Sure, that sounds like a good idea."

Three pings sounded in rapid succession. Riley was a man of no frills on his technology. But he'd given Lucy her own text tone years ago. The only one to ever have that distinction. He plucked the phone from his back pocket and tapped open the text.

Are you two interested in sledding?

He didn't want to interrupt George's sharing or his gift for his mother. Riley typed back, careful to keep George from thinking he'd stopped paying attention.

How about you go ahead and gather up his snow gear. We'll join you when we finish up.

Lucy trudged up the hill alongside George, who was riding on the sled while Riley pulled him to the top. At this rate, she was going to wear herself out with all this memory making, taking away any energy for temptation.

Although she and Riley hadn't discussed that kiss, she felt confident he was mirroring her all the same. That they were piling event onto event to keep from risking a repeat before they could sort out their feelings.

And this day was sure cold enough to freeze away any heated thoughts.

Two staff members sat waiting on snowmobiles

in case someone needed assistance. Icy snowflakes drifted lazily from plump winter clouds. The sunshine of the morning had been exchanged for a horizon of winter white.

Her gaze moved back to Riley's broad shoulders as he pulled the sled. She couldn't bear to lose his friendship. He'd been her best friend since he'd come strutting into her freshman homeroom class.

The other girls had been drooling over his country-boy twang and swagger. She'd been drawn to the ache in his eyes, a hurt that she'd later found out came from leaving behind a farm lifestyle because his addict father had run out of work options everywhere else. The family had to follow him while he accepted a job in the city. She'd seen the grief and loss stamped on Riley's face. A loneliness echoed in her own heart as the new kid who'd relocated at the start of the year with her mom after her parents' divorce.

Huffing up the hill, she hoped Riley would see this simpler outing—together—sledding as an olive branch. Watching families and lovers send their sleds careening down, Lucy searched for something to say. Conversation had always been so easy for them. She missed that ease. "Now *this* is Christmassy."

Riley chuckled, his laugh sending a puffy white

cloud into the freezing-cold air. "Look at the happy faces of all those people excited because their children will be worn out at the end of the day."

George was certainly all in, dancing in the snow, then flopping down on his back to make a snow angel.

As they moved up the hill, closer to the top and their turn, she pointed to the older couple climbing onto a sled together. "That's Patsy and Lonnie. They are the ranch's massage therapists. They also teach classes in mixing essential oils."

"Jacob has pulled together quite a staff."

Lucy let loose words she'd held tightly in her chest all day long. "Are you and I talking again?"

For a moment, she swore she could see those words frozen in the space and silence between them.

He paused before answering, "I didn't think we'd stopped."

She was too tired to pretend, and she'd thought their friendship was strong enough they shouldn't have to. "Then why are you avoiding me? If there's a problem, or if you're having regrets," she lowered her voice, "George and I can leave. It's okay to change your mind. I can word things so he doesn't know the difference."

Even as she offered, she knew she would be hurt

beyond measure if he took her up on the offer to cut the trip short.

"I haven't changed my mind," he said somberly, not even a hint of doubt in his words.

She held on to his arm under the guise of keeping her balance, her gaze holding his every bit as firmly. "This just isn't as simple as we expected."

A flash of understanding, of connection passed between them. Her friend was back. But with that came the inescapable truth that their bond of friendship might not be strong enough to carry them through whatever had changed between them this week.

George jumped up and down, tugging her sleeve and drawing her back into the present. "Come on, Mommy. Let's go, let's go, let's gooooooo."

And then heaven help her, as she settled onto the sled with her son in front of her, Riley pushed the tandem sled. Faster and faster. Then he hopped on behind her, sitting, all man, all around her until crashing was the least of her worries.

Sledding with Lucy and George had made for a top-notch, happy holiday memory.

Except now, on their last night together before George would leave with his father, Riley needed to find a time to tell Lucy about his conversation with George during the elves' workshop. Time was running out—and he would tell her, soon. He didn't want anything to taint this memory for her or for George.

This moment was one-hundred-percent about the wonder of Christmas. And *wonder* was the right word as they waited for Santa to make an appearance, rappelling off a cliff.

The outside space was built into a mountain, the side sheared off. Jacob had told him they sometimes used it for drive-in movie evenings. Not tonight, though.

A spotlight clicked on, splashing across the mountainside, sweeping, searching, until it landed on...

Santa Claus?

The beam steadied on the man in a red suit rappelling down the mountainside, a red sack slung over his shoulder, swaying in the wind. A large sleigh waited below with two massive Clydesdale horses.

The children squealed with excitement and Riley had to confess, it took his mind off his worries. Santa made his way down, closer and closer to the sleigh waiting at the bottom in such a fun and unique display.

In the soft multicolor glow, Riley stole a glance

at Lucy. His best friend had her hands shoved into her parka's pockets, face framed by a plaid scarf, a smile digging dimples into her cheeks that were flush from the cold.

A mirror image from earlier today when her body had been nestled in front of him—a thought threatened to melt the snow right off his hat.

Then the loudspeaker crackled a moment's warning before Santa's voice boomed through the loudspeaker. A hush fell over the crowd as the kids leaned forward, eyes wide with anticipation. "Have all you boys been very, very good this year?"

A cheer rippled through the crowd.

Santa continued, "And what about all the girls? Have you been very, very good, as well?"

A louder cheer swelled from the female guests.

Santa raised his hands. "Gentlemen, I think the ladies have you beat. Do you want to try again?"

The competition went back and forth, boys and girls, cheering about having behaved until finally Old Saint Nick clapped his hands. "I think you all have been the best of girls and boys, and I have a present for each of you waiting here in my sleigh."

A collective squeal of delight went through the children, the whole group moving toward the sleigh where elves waited to keep an orderly line.

Lucy turned to Riley, looking up. "I know this

was in the registration packet, but no line item description could do this justice. I've never seen anything like it. And all those gifts..."

"That was a part of the registration, as well. We were given a list of items to choose from for the children. I was impressed by the way the presents were roughly the same price and size so that no child will get more than another." He appreciated that detail.

Christmas had been tough for him even after the holiday season was over. Upon returning to school, he would have to listen to all the other kids talk about their perfect family time and how Santa showered them with presents because they were so good. At that age, it had been rough understanding why Santa loved him less than Peter Williams who got detention for cutting off a girl's pigtails and punching a kid two years younger.

"What did you choose for George?"

"You mean what did Saint Nicholas pick?" he asked, quirking an eyebrow directing her attention back forward. "You'll have to wait and see."

Wind ruffled the manes on Santa's horses. Jolly Old Saint Nick stooped, pulling exquisitely wrapped gifts from his bag. Children assembled in a line, the awe of the moment shining on their faces. Every child was given their gift, a hug and a picture with Santa Claus.

Did Lucy realize she was leaning back against his chest? Riley didn't bother stopping himself, didn't even care to wonder why he wasn't thinking about Emily, he just circled an arm around Lucy's waist and pulled her closer. Her body tensed against him for an instant, then she relaxed into him.

Another bracing gust of wind had Riley slipping up his jacket's Sherpa collar. A move he was hesitant to make, afraid of puncturing the strange peace and excitement that filled him now. Or of having Lucy pull away.

"Mommy, Mommy, look," George called out, trudging through a patch of snow clutching a large rectangular package covered in snowman wrapping paper. With eager hands, George tore open the present while Lucy bent over to snag wrapping paper before it flew away.

Hand covering his mouth, George jumped up and down. In his right hand, a Lego garbage truck. George held the toy, studying the box with avid eyes.

"Santa heard me," he said with wonder. "He heard."

It was a good thing to be heard in life. For life to be happy and fair. The joy on George's face, echoed on Lucy's, was absolute perfection. It felt so rewarding to see the pleasure in her eyes after being at odds most of the day, to know that he'd played at least a small part in putting that joy there.

And there was no way that their new accord would hold up to the harsh light of day tomorrow. Saying goodbye to George.

Facing time alone with Lucy, no distractions to provide a buffer from their shifting relationship.

Chapter Seven

"Star of wonder..."

The tune hummed softly through the outdoor sound system, a fitting serenade for an evening of stargazing. Fireworks were scheduled to begin in a half hour.

Pushing back worries about tomorrow—of her son leaving, of being alone with Riley and all this new tension between them—Lucy tucked her knees to her chest, sitting on the outdoor lounger under the night sky. Outdoor heaters had been set up around the patio for guests who wanted to brave the elements and stargaze. The hum of Riley's low voice flowed over her like warm Irish coffee.

On the other side of the glass doors, children clustered on a rug for story time with Mrs. Claus reading and elves acting out the scenes. George wore his footed plaid pj's. It was the perfect end to a packed full day.

Except Lucy was totally and completely freaking out.

She should be feeling happy because of the family atmosphere, but she knew the family atmosphere between Riley and her was just make-believe with him as a stand-in father figure. Was she providing enough for George on her own the rest of the time, given how special this getaway with Riley felt?

Regardless, she wanted to save the good memories forever. But it wasn't like she could take this jumble of emotions and sort them in a binder. She was stuck smack-dab in the middle of her messy feelings. Could others tell she felt like a fraud?

Couples and families occupied chairs and tables spread out on the large patio, each grouping set up for privacy. She hugged her new blanket around her, each stamped message all the more special because George had chosen them. He'd been so proud to present his gift to her after supper, declaring he'd waited all day for the ink to dry and that Santa's elves had sewn them together. He'd given Riley a ceramic horse that she'd helped him paint before they came to the ranch. They'd all exchanged presents in the past, but this was their first holiday doing so where she and Riley were both unattached.

It was…surreal.

Turning to Riley, soaking in the sight of his strong profile, Lucy tucked the blanket under her chin. "This was such a sweet gift. I thought for sure he would make me a toy train—which I would have cherished, of course. But this? He thought of what would mean the most to me, rather than what he would want. I know he's rowdy, but he's also such a sweet child."

Riley stretched his legs out, crossing his feet at the ankles, boots catching a few flakes of snow. "He gets that from his mama. I still have the quilt you crocheted for me in high school."

"Seriously? How did I not know that?" Back in high school when she still had braces perfecting her smile, she'd given him the blanket. Soft yarn of blue and green—his favorite colors. Her first big craft project, and the only one she'd ever given as a gift.

"You've never been in my bedroom."

The innuendo hung between them in a loading moment, before she averted her eyes, tracing a finger over the symbol for hope. Starlight above seemed to glow brighter. "Well, uhm, I'm surprised the blanket held together. My craft skills were—and are—negligible at best."

"It's my napping blanket."

His fingers were barely a breath from her. A phantom touch sent anticipatory shivers down her spine.

"Then I'm definitely surprised it hasn't worn out yet." She risked a glance at him, hoping her attempt at humor would bring back the ease to their friendship. She missed it. Missed him.

He chuckled—thank goodness—and she relaxed into her seat, resting her head against the back to study the clear night sky.

Riley cleared his throat. "I think you should know that George and I had an interesting conversation while you were gone from Santa's workshop."

Peace skittered away at the serious tone in his voice, leaving her chilled. "What did he say?"

"He asked to take Pickles with him to his father's house. He said he was worried Pickles would be scared without him."

She squeezed her eyes closed for just a moment, tears burning. She knew all too well that her son was giving them a glimpse into his own fears. "I hate this. I hate it—I hate it. He's four years old."

She blinked back the tears and looked back to him. "I wish Colin would have taken me up on the offer for us all to spend Christmas together."

"You did what?" His eyes flared, bright like the constellations overhead. Searching her face as tension worked to furrow his brow and sharpen his jawline.

Casting her eyes upward, starward, she drew in a deep breath, hoping to draw some strength from the night sky the same way she had when they were young. When serious moments rumbled in the distance of their conversations.

Lucy counted to three. Willed her voice to be strong. Fixed as Polaris. "I offered it last year too when it was my turn to have George at Christmas, but he said no then and now. Trust me, I don't want to spend the holidays with Colin either, but I thought it might make things easier on George. But Colin disagrees with me."

"Ah, man, Lucy," he said, his voice cracking as he angled over to wrap her in a hug.

And she couldn't stop herself from sinking into the comfort of his embrace, her cheek resting against the warm strength of his chest. More than anything, she wanted to tip her face up and kiss him. If the spark would kindle all the brighter with her wrapped in a blanket of hope.

Was she imagining the heat of his breath against the top of her head? Were his hands moving along her back in comfort…or something else?

Tomorrow, when her son left with his father, Lucy would have to face those questions, regardless of the answer.

Thumbing his phone onto Silent, Riley ignored the text message from Emily and tossed his cell onto the kitchen counter. His ex was the last person he wanted to hear from today. It was Christmas Eve. The day he and Emily had planned to say their vows.

He knew without a doubt now that they were wrong for each other, but that didn't erase the frustration from how things had shaken out between them. He just wanted to get through the rest of the day, starting with this shared breakfast with George.

Muffled sounds from the next room drifted through the door as Lucy packed the last of her son's clothes. Riley shoveled another bite of French toast into his mouth.

For those who preferred a family morning over spending Christmas Eve in the ranch's dining room, the staff had delivered breakfast casseroles to be stored in the refrigerator overnight. George had chosen the French toast casserole with warm maple syrup.

Already having seconds, the kid washed down another bite with a gulp of milk, then set down his favorite superhero cup and swiped the milk moustache that had formed on his lip. "Thank you for bringing us here so we could see Santa Claus."

"Absolutely, tiger. Thanks for coming with me. You've made my Christmas the best ever." As he said the words, he was surprised to realize how true they were. Which didn't seem possible, given this should have been his honeymoon. But there was something magical about this past week, thanks to George...and Lucy.

"What did you ask Santa Claus to bring you for Christmas?" George forked up another bite of French toast. The boy's bright eyes twinkled in the firelight, his face earnest and interested.

Nothing? "It's a secret."

George clapped a hand over his heart and whispered, "I won't tell."

While pouring a fresh pool of syrup, Riley scavenged for something to tell the boy, because truthfully, he had no idea what he wanted anymore. "Okay, I'd like a pan of your mom's brownies."

"They're the best," the little guy agreed, his legs swinging. George balanced his syrup-covered fork on his pointer finger for a moment, before grabbing the utensil tightly again and stabbing another piece. "Does she let you have a spoonful of frosting? You gotta ask her before she uses it all up."

"I'll remember that." He pulled a smile, his gaze shifting to the photo on the refrigerator of the three of them wearing matching plaid-and-reindeer Christmas pj's in front of a tree.

The snapshot had been a part of the Top Dog package. George's delight in the picture as evident as the coal smile on the snowman the three of them had created in front of the cabin. From where Riley sat, he could make out the grinning snowman with a button nose and green paisley scarf, just outside the window. Lucy built the base of the snowman by the fir tree in the front lawn so, as she said, the multicolor-lit Christmas tree wouldn't be lonely for the holidays.

"Riley, but you still haven't told me what do you want from Santa?" He overenunciated each syllable as if Riley somehow hadn't understood. "Not from Mom. From *Santa*."

The boy was persistent. No doubt.

"How about I tell you what I wanted as a kid?"

George pursed his lips together. Considering. Then nodded until his hair tumbled onto his forehead. "Okay."

Riley's mind skated back to that Christmas about two decades ago. "I wanted a horse."

The boy's mouth formed an ohh, his eyes wide, his attention rapt. "Did you get it?"

"Not exactly." Looking back, it had been a mighty big ask given how little money his folks had. "But I got riding lessons."

His mom had taken on extra hours at the day care where she worked. That had been his happiest holiday memory as a kid before his family imploded.

George set down his fork solemnly. "Santa's not going to know where to find me."

"Of course, he will. Santa knows everything."

"But I'm with my mom sometimes and with my dad sometimes." His eyebrows pinched together in a deep frown. "My mom tells me where I'm going to be and when I'm going, but it's still hard to remember. What if Santa comes here looking for me?"

He thought they'd put this worry to rest for George. Apparently not. "I promise, Santa won't forget you."

"But what if he leaves my stuff here?"

"Then your mom and I will bring it to you."

George nudged the last bite of breakfast around on his plate in the way he did when he was thinking through something. Then nodded. "Thank you for making sure my mommy's not alone on Christmas."

"I'll make sure she's okay and that Santa knows exactly where to find her too." Riley cupped the kid's head and tousled his curls, his heart full of love for this little boy.

George and Lucy were such an integral part of his life, he didn't know what he would do if that was taken away. He might not know what he wanted for Christmas, but he sure knew what he absolutely did not want.

He didn't want this child to be hurt by another person he had every right to depend on. Riley understood too well how those childhood scars stayed with a person, whether it was the times his father had been a no-show or the other times he'd been so very toxically, drunkenly present. Even though he didn't have his father's challenges with addiction, Riley would not let history repeat itself by letting down people he cared about.

Which meant he had one week left here at the Top Dog Dude Ranch, alone with Lucy, to figure out where their friendship was going. Failure was not an option.

Lucy plastered a smile on her face as Colin's car pulled up to the cabin, the sparkling new Mercedes sedan parking beside her van. The only thing she could control? Trying to make the handoff of George to his dad as calm as possible. If she was upset, George would be all the more unsettled.

Ragged breaths punctuated her steps from the porch ledge to the path of fresh powdery snow. George kept pace with her as they moved down the walkway to the parking area. Their boots pressed new tracks into snow.

George paused for a moment, head tipping toward the well-decorated Christmas tree next to the snowman they'd made after sledding. Memories shuffled through, adding to so many from this trip, of gathering the materials, the impromptu snowball fight. Each moment danced in Lucy's mind as she followed her son's gaze.

"Hey, Frosty." George waved to the snowman, his eyes lighting with holiday magic. "Merry Christmas."

How she wanted to freeze this moment and not move into the next. Lucy wrapped her arms around herself, the wool jacket snug against her body. With a deep exhale, she tried to soothe her fraying sense of control, sending a cloud of breath into the winter air.

She looked beyond Colin's car, out toward the houses tucked into the snowy hillside, as if she could somehow distance herself. Even from here, she marked the movement of her neighbors as filled with joy. She heard laughter on the wind, noticed the way families gathered and tossed snowballs at each other. Real joy sparked in the family grabbing sleds for an outing, all while she was struggling to hold it together.

It was all she could do to hide her nerves and frustration. She'd done her best at pretending to eat the French toast casserole. When she couldn't fake it any longer, she'd made the excuse of needing to pack…something she'd already completed during the sleepless night.

Earlier in the week, the other moms on the playground had tried to make light of her worries, saying how they would be grateful for a week away from their kids. She knew they didn't mean to hurt her, but the comments made her angry all the same. It wasn't like she had a choice with this.

And she certainly didn't want to be away from her child over Christmas.

She took another lurching step forward as the exhaust of the black Mercedes billowed into frigid air. An hour ago, snow dusted the view in front of her cabin. Clean, untarnished pillows of white had glittered in the morning sunlight as she'd packed George's bags. Now the gritty gray tire tracks disturbed the pristine vision and her fragile sense of peace.

She felt exposed in the harsh, reflective sunlight, as if under a microscope. The way the day surely illuminated the wear on her secondhand wool jacket. Showed the years in her favorite pair of snow boots. A stark contrast to Colin as he exited the luxury car. His fitted leather jacket glistened, his body sporting a gym-rat quality that she would bet her last dollar didn't come with any real-life calluses. Wind ruffled his floppy blond hair that curled out from under a charcoal-gray wool newsboy cap.

How had she been fooled by him? So taken in by appearances?

At least he hadn't married the woman he cheated with while George was being born. That would have made the handoff all the more difficult. After all that betrayal, he'd ended up marrying someone else.

Talia stayed in the vehicle, waving. She rolled down the window and called out, "Merry Christmas, Lucy. I'm just going to sit tight in here while y'all take care of the details. I wouldn't want to get in the way."

Lucy waved back, determined to be polite even though it was so strange to hand her child over to a person who wouldn't even make small talk. "Merry Christmas to you, as well."

Riley carried the suitcase. She started to follow, then doubled back to snag a gift bag and George's new Lego garbage truck. She picked her way down the cabin steps, careful not to slip.

Colin kept his hands in his wool coat pockets, his eyes wary around her even after all this time. "Good morning, Lucy. Merry Christmas."

Was it? Not really. But she smiled anyway. "And to you. I hope your drive was uneventful."

"Good weather and cleared roads the whole way," he said with a thin smile, all gusto and no heart.

How strange to exchange such banal pleasantries with someone she'd once vowed to love for the rest of her life. "I hope you'll have the same going back. Please do let me know when you've arrived safely."

She started to pass over the truck.

Colin shook his head dismissively. "He won't need that."

Her heart clenched. She didn't want to bring any tension to an already stressful exchange, but this was about George, a child. Their child. "He just got it for Christmas. He'll want to play with it in the car."

Still, Colin kept his hands in his coat pockets,

not making any move to take the toy. "Talia has made him a bag of toys and treats to keep him occupied until we get home. If you hold on to that, we won't have to bother finding it later and transporting it back to you."

She pulled yet another tight smile. The last thing she wanted—or that George needed—was tension in the air from an argument.

"Alright, if you insist." She plucked out her notebook, finding much needed peace in the organization. Her fingertips, numbing from the cold, brushed the graphic organizer she'd made for the trip. "Because you haven't seen him since November, I've typed up all the latest on his bedtime routine and a few reminders on foods he doesn't like right now—"

"Oh, we won't have problems with food. He won't starve." He glanced back over his shoulder to look at Talia who pressed a phone to her ear, stoplight red lips arching into a laugh at an unheard conversation.

She clenched her teeth. She knew that odds were Colin and Talia would go out of their way to shower him with all of his favorites. But the dismissal of her input as a parent grated.

"Well, here's the list in case you need it. I'll email it to you and Talia, as well." She extended the paper to him and he snatched it from her with a force that surprised her.

"So organized. As always."

She knew, knew, knew he probably hadn't meant anything by the statement and that she was only feeling prickly over saying goodbye to her son at Christmas. But it was all she could do not to snap at him. She clamped her jaws shut tighter and passed a bag of gifts.

Colin frowned. "He has plenty from us. You can hold on to those until you see him again."

"These are gifts he chose for you and Talia."

At least Colin had the decency to look chagrined for being rude. And possibly because he clearly hadn't thought to do the same for her in return.

She'd taken George to a ceramics shop for a special mommy-and-son morning out. He'd chosen items to paint as gifts—and made the horse for Riley. He'd picked a pencil holder for his dad and a jewelry dish for Talia. He'd concentrated so intently on painting each one. She hoped that Colin would show all sorts of excitement and appreciation, that he wouldn't hurt her little boy's feelings.

Colin took the bag and passed it through the window to Talia, then clapped his gloves together. "Alright, George, let's load up so we get home in time for Christmas Eve supper with your family."

Riley stepped up, George holding on to his hand. Her son clasped her hand too, his bottom lip quivery. He looked so small in his blue snowsuit, a fraction of his extroverted self from yesterday, taking the sledding hill with full-on enthusiasm. Building the snowman afterward. The paisley scarf on Frosty stirred in the wind.

Deep blue eyes searched hers. "Mommy? Why can't we all stay here? Riley, can't you ask them too?"

She knelt in front of her son, brushing back his red curls. "George, sweetie, we've talked through this. You're going to spend Christmas with your daddy and Talia. You'll do all sorts of fun things together. You can call me every day, anytime." She pressed a kiss to his forehead. "I love you."

Tears welled in his eyes as he looked up at his father. "Daddy, I want to stay here with my mommy."

"Champ, it's time for us to go." Colin hefted up George and started walking to the car. No warning. No attempt to calm his son. "Talia, pop the trunk so they can load his things."

Lucy held on to her control by a thread.

"Mommy…" George wailed with his arms extended for her.

Her breath hitched, her throat clogging with emotion. She searched for some way to make this better, but Colin was already strapping George into his car seat. As each of her son's cries grew louder and louder, she grew madder and madder.

Why couldn't Colin take even five minutes to make this easier? Or he could have accepted her offer to share breakfast to make the transition more gradual, while giving George a blended family memory?

Legally, there wasn't a thing she could do. It was Colin's right to have this Christmas with George.

But she would sure feel better about it if he would show some parental compassion.

Holding on by a thread, she kept her own tears at bay, blowing her son a kiss as the car pulled away. His sobs showing no signs of easing.

Only when the taillights faded from sight did she realize that Riley had put his arms around her. Without hesitation, she turned to bury her face in his chest, letting all her grief come pouring out.

Chapter Eight

Watching the taillights fade from view on Colin's Mercedes sedan, Riley hugged Lucy close, her body shaking against him. He clenched his fists against her back, struggling to regain control of his own anger, grief. George's cries echoed in his mind so tangibly he could swear they carried on the morning wind, threading sorrow through the trees until it created a web of icy pain.

She dragged in a ragged breath; her face dipped as she stepped back, shaking out her hands. "Give me a minute. I need...to breathe. To walk it out."

Nodding tightly, he gave her space. He wouldn't

mind taking a beat himself, to pull himself together so he could be there for her the way she needed.

Lucy had played along nicely during the exchange, but Riley had struggled not to tell the jerk off for a list of reasons too long to name… For starters, though? How dare the guy make such a big deal out of all he could give George when Lucy was the one doing the heavy lifting every day. No wonder George was afraid of change. Colin canceled half the time.

But right now wasn't about Colin. And it wasn't about Riley either. Lucy was George's mother, the best mother Riley had ever seen, and she had to be torn apart by her son's cries.

A thump startled him. He pivoted fast, instincts honed from a lifetime atop horses, just in time to see a snowball hit the side of the cabin.

Lucy scooped up snow and hurled another missile, and another. Her jaw went tighter with each toss, her anger—her sadness—building momentum until it was nearly palpable. Her snow cannons exploded on impact against the wood grooves.

In the years he and Lucy had been friends, he could barely recall times he'd seen her angry. Now rage radiated off her as she unleashed a bevy of tightly packed snowballs at her opponent, the cabin.

Green eyes were no longer inflected with the grace of gentle fields. Instead, they darkened.

This snowball fight against an enemy-by-proxy, taking her normally well-contained frustration out by tossing it at the log wall. At least all the other families in nearby cabins had long disappeared, the mountainside quiet. The privacy offered a small thing to be grateful for in the middle of a horrible morning.

"I hate this," she said between gritted teeth. "I absolutely hate it for my child. I tried so hard to do everything right, and still it turned out all wrong and my son is the one paying the price."

He raked up another snowball for her, packing it tight, grateful for the outlet for his own frustration. "Here you go."

Her arms fell to her sides; she was looking so defeated as she stared at the snowball for a long moment. "I don't want to be angry." She clenched her fists, ice on her red mittens crackling. "I swore I would do this coparenting thing right for George's sake."

"And you are." He took one of her hands in his and pressed the snowball into her palm. "You're being far nicer to Colin than he deserves. You have a right to be angry. George is nowhere in sight to witness this. Vent away."

Her chin quivered, then steadied, fire lighting her eyes. She hauled back and launched the icy missile at a fat oak tree. Then spun to look for another target. She kicked the snowman they'd built earlier. But their Frosty was sturdier than that. It held strong, stayed tall.

Riley took a step back, then launched a roundhouse kick at the snowman. "Come on, Lucy, have at it. No judgment. It's just us out here."

Like it had been for well over a decade.

"Just us," she echoed, turning slowly to face him, her scarf sliding to the ground, cheeks pink from the cold. She extended a hand to him.

He reached, clasped. And without another thought, drew her to his chest. She curled against him and held on tightly this time. Her body shook with silent sobs that threatened to tear him in half. He rubbed his hands along her back, offering a bunch of nonsensical words he hoped helped. He doubted it, though.

But he tried. "I'm here, Lucy. You can hold on to me as long as you like. It's going to be okay. You'll miss him, but he will be back before you know it. He loves you and he knows he's loved…"

She tipped her face toward him. Silently. Staring up, the ever-present connection between them never stronger. He stroked her hair from her face, a strand catching along tears on her cheek.

Unable to resist, he dipped his head and pressed his mouth to hers.

Lucy went still for all of three seconds, long enough to throw caution to the wind and pour her hurt, pain, grief into kissing Riley. Into the draw that had been growing exponentially during this surreal Christmas vacation that jumbled up revelry and loss into a snarl more persistent than tangled holiday lights.

She flung off her mittens and thrust her hands under his hat, combed her fingers through his hair. How could she have not known it wasn't coarse, but rather thick and soft and she wanted to lose herself in the texture?

Lose herself in him.

She arched against him, savoring the press of their bodies, even through layers of winter clothing. She skimmed her hands down to his face, then traveled into his jacket. Her fingers ached to discover more of him, to distance herself from the heartache of the morning, to fill the longtime void of loneliness by exploring the attraction between them.

Was he easing back? Every cell in her cried out in denial. Twisting her grip in his coat, she drew him nearer, steering their steps closer to the cabin, toward the inviting getaway just beyond that door.

Riley planted his boots in the snow. Immovable.

The passion sizzling through her veins cooled, reason returning. She inched back to look in his eyes. "Riley? What's wrong?"

He scooped his hat from the ground and passed over her mittens. "I should be comforting you, not kissing you. That was insensitive of me. I'm sorry. You know the last thing I would ever want to do is take advantage of you."

"You have nothing to apologize for," she insisted, taking her mittens from him, hating the awkwardness between them, so alien for their relationship she had no idea how to handle it. This was Riley. Her best friend. She couldn't lose that. "If anything, I should ask your forgiveness. I should have remembered that this was supposed to be your honeymoon. You were going to get married today."

"Thank heaven I didn't," he mumbled under his breath as he stepped over the remains of their snowman on his way to the porch.

The ache in his voice was unmistakable. She needed to do better at comforting him, empathizing. She certainly understood the pain of rejection. "Even knowing it is right to be out of a bad relationship, it still hurts. It's hard not to grieve over what could have been, what we wished happened—like how I wanted George to have the best from life."

Walking with him step for step—so many times, they faced pain side by side—she entered the cabin, the space so unbearably quiet without George. From the plush leather chair next to the quiet, rolling fire, Pickles let out a chuff. His scruffy face quirking to the side before he leaped off.

Though small, the dog knew how to hustle.

Little flecks of snow slid from Lucy's boots to the ground. Pickles sniffed and licked the ice before leaning against her legs. Sensing, she felt, that she needed puppy cuddles. After scooping up the dog in her arms, she cradled him close against her chest. Pickles planted a wet lick across her cheek, tail wagging so hard his whole body wriggled.

"You have to know that George *has* the best." Riley closed the door behind him. "He has you."

His compliment soothed the raw wound inside her. She valued Riley's opinion so very much. More than anyone else's.

Too much, perhaps?

"I'm sorry for being so wrapped up in myself that I didn't notice you and Emily were struggling." She kicked off her boots and slipped out of her jacket, although no amount of busying herself could help her avoid the question knocking around inside her. "Does our friendship interfere with finding that forever relationship?"

He hung his jacket on the coat tree with slow deliberation before turning to face her, leaning back against the door with his arms crossed.

"Emily was jealous of our friendship." He met her gaze steady on. "I also know that you gave her no cause to be jealous."

She cradled the dog in her arms to keep from reaching for Riley. "That's rather ironic, considering we just kissed each other."

"Point taken," he said with a nod before finally stepping away. He adjusted the flame on the electric fireplace by the Christmas tree that had an empty spot underneath where George's gifts had been but now rested forlorn by the door.

She exhaled long and hard, still unable to let herself off the hook so easily for kissing Riley. Or rather, for returning his kiss. "Even if we somehow were able to take things to a 'friends with benefits' level, it couldn't be today. Not on what should be your wedding day."

And whoa, why did she have to keep circling back around to that thought? Perhaps because it was a big deal and she shouldn't need to keep reminding herself. What a selfish friend she was today, thinking only of her own pain.

He angled his head toward her, a wry look on his face. "Friends with benefits?"

Whoops.

Had she really said that? More important, had she meant it? Either way, she would need more time to figure that out. To decide if she could risk staying here for the remaining week or if she needed to run like crazy back home.

No matter what, she wasn't bailing on him during Christmas. "It's just a saying." She tried to brush aside the notion of a phrase she never should have uttered. "Are we still going to the ugly Christmas sweater party and holiday hoedown? Because if so, I really need to get changed."

She didn't bother waiting for an answer but avoided his eyes on her way to the bedroom. She gripped the doorknob just as his voice stopped her.

"Lucy?"

"Yes?" she answered without turning.

"I'm sorry I didn't speak up about Colin sooner. I always had a bad feeling about him."

Turning, she let herself look at him, her friend, whose face carried far too much worry and guilt.

"Riley, that wasn't your place to tell me then." She should have figured it out for herself. "And even if you had spoken up, I wouldn't have listened."

"You might have."

"Perhaps." She did value his opinion, trusted him more than anyone else. But if she believed that, then she would have to ask herself why she hadn't mentioned her apprehension about Emily. And she already knew that answer. Because she was afraid of losing Riley's friendship.

Something that still hadn't changed. Which made her feel even more ridiculous than when she'd tried on the ugly sweater she bought for the holiday hoedown.

There were so many thoughts to churn around and at such an already emotional time, given the pain of George leaving... And her kiss with Riley. She didn't trust herself to sort it out today.

Instead, she set herself on the mission of having fun the way they used to before life got so complicated.

Riley shoveled snow from the demolished snowman, working to clear the pathway from the cabin before Lucy came out for the ugly Christmas sweater party. The afternoon event would be followed by a holiday hoedown. He could have called the main desk to have the path cleared, but quite frankly, he needed the release that good old-fashioned manual labor would bring.

Pickles let out a little yip, and Riley stepped over to make sure the puppy gate was secure. Pickles pranced over to nudge Riley's gloved hand. Tongue lazily sliding out of the side of the dog's mouth, Pickles enjoyed the ear scratches.

Riley was glad to have Lucy here with him on the vacation, but he hadn't expected it to be so complicated. He'd thought his heart had been ripped out by Emily. But today's events had taken heartache to a whole new level.

He returned to shoveling just as a movement at the edge of the sloping winter hill caught his attention. A doe darted from the tree line. Pickles jumped up, ears perked forward as he bounded toward the safety gate closing off the patio. His scruffy face pushed against the wood slats, his whole body shaking in interest.

"Easy, buddy," Riley muttered, watching the doe bound across the snow. The easy grace of the animal made for a stark contrast with Pickles's antics and his own unease on the day.

George wasn't his child. He understood that. But it didn't stop the urge to protect the kid and he'd never trusted Colin, not even back in the time before he'd proven himself to be a faithless, cheating jerk…

* * *

Riley swept off his Stetson, heart still thudding from the rush of the gallop after the last rounded barrel. The announcer on the crackling PA system broke the buzz of the crowd.

"Riley on Windsail has done it, folks! He's won and more than that—he just shattered our record for the fastest time in this arena."

Reaching to pat his pinto gelding on the neck, he engaged in the silent exchange of thanks with his horse. All the while, he scanned the crowd. Hoping to find Lucy. There was no one in the world he wanted to celebrate with and talk to more than her, his best friend.

Normally, her wildfire red hair allowed him to pick her out of any group. She usually waited close to the arena despite her lingering fear of horses. He'd always given her credit for that. He sifted through the clamor of activity as folks mounted and dismounted.

There. He saw her in faded blue jeans and a white-and-black-plaid button-up. She shot him a thumbs-up, joy pulling sunshine into the peaks of her face. But she made no move to come closer.

Instead, her new fiancé, Colin, hustled over. "Congratulations on your win. I guess this was a lucky week for both of us. Lucy is quite a prize."

Prize? More like a treasure. Riley pulled a tight smile, hands flexing along the oiled leather reins. "As long as Lucy's happy, I'm happy. Congrats to you both."

"Thanks, we appreciate that," Colin answered, while tipping his spiffy new, never-worn-before Stetson at a tall slender woman with country-road curves as she walked by. Shifting his attention back, Colin cleared his throat, pulling his mouth into something between a smile and a grimace. "I was worried at first that there was something going on between the two of you."

A roar from the crowd as one of the junior competitors masterfully navigated a dark bay mare through an obstacle course. Riley's attention diverted from Colin for a brief moment, just in time to see the young girl's face light with triumph.

Riley leaned forward on his black show saddle's horn, reins gathered in his left hand. "You needn't have worried. I'm on the road all the time and when you two met, I was seeing Nora Jean."

"That didn't mean you and Lucy weren't...you know." He leaned closer, his voice low and rumbling as a summer storm, his pale eyes deadly serious.

"No. I'm afraid I don't." Riley straightened in the saddle. Jaw flexing into anger, teeth grind-

ing. He wanted to like this guy. He really did. But Colin was making it a challenge. "To be clear, I don't care for the insinuation that Lucy or I would be the type to cheat. That's the lowest of the low."

Colin held up his hands defensively. "Okay, okay. No offense meant." He paused. The gulf between them roared as loud as the crowd—but not in a good way. Colin cleared his throat. "And this is where you're supposed to say, No offense taken."

Windsail shifted uneasily. Stamped his hoof on the clay ground. Splattering arena dirt on Colin's dark blue jeans.

Riley smoothed a hand along his horse's neck while he pinned Colin with an icy stare. "Just be good to Lucy."

Knowing he should take his own advice from that day long ago, Riley jabbed the shovel into the snow, but it did nothing to ease the anger still building up inside. Most of it was directed at himself. Because he should have known better than to trust Lucy to Colin. The evidence had been there right from the start. The man was an idiot. And there wasn't anything more Riley could do to protect her from Colin now than he had then.

Pickles, having lost interest once the doe had bounded into the woods, sat patiently watching.

His dark eyes turned joyful as Riley reached over the porch gate to pet him again.

"If only things were as simple as this, Pickles. You have no idea how hard it is to be a person."

But as sure as he'd been clearing away the demolished snowman, he would do everything he could to clear the way for Lucy to have the future she deserved. After his talk with Lucy, he knew he should have spoken up back then, despite her saying she wouldn't have listened. He saw now he had a right to speak up as her best friend, and someone who knew her well. He wouldn't let her fall into a position with a man who would leave her pelting the cabin with snowballs again. No one would get past him this time—especially not a guy like Colin who was all show and no substance.

Lucy deserved better.

"Ho, ho, ho, welcome to the Holiday Hoedown."

Lucy knew she needed to move away from the entryway if she wanted to stop hearing the greeting repeated every time a new guest walked into the party.

Nibbling a gingerbread-man cookie decorated with a frosting sweater, Lucy appreciated that Riley was trying hard to help distract her from being sad over her first Christmas alone. He certainly had a knack for being there when she needed him.

But even she couldn't have predicted the lengths to which he would go to help her this Christmas Eve. Any other time, she would have been all in on this party.

Riley's ugly sweater still made Lucy grin. A bay horse was centered on his torso with a light-up Santa hat on the ears. Alternating patterns of text that read in all caps Horsey Holidays and horseshoes provided the backdrop for the horse head.

And somehow, he managed to make it look sexy. Probably because he never took himself too seriously.

Dark hair shining under the strands of lights strung overhead, Riley was deep in conversation with Jacob whose ugly sweater was far milder featuring a beagle driving a sleigh. They waved over Douglas Archer, Jacob's new business partner and dairy farmer. His green ugly sweater sported a Holstein cow holding a plate of milk and Christmas cookies.

Country takes on Christmas classics reverberated in the oversize barn where adults sipped on spiked hot chocolate and the smattering of teens and older children opted for the customizable hot-chocolate bar with the gourmet marshmallows in every shape and flavor infusion.

Incandescent string lights wrapped around a fir and garland hung from the ceilings, making the red barn seem elegant and brimming with Christmas cheer. Folks registered for the ugly-sweater contest while others piled their plates high from the spread of holiday-themed finger food ranging from barbecue meatballs to jalapeño cheese poppers.

In the far corner of the bar, a line had formed for Santa Limbo. Santa and Mrs. Claus held and lowered the limbo stick while laughter roared.

The couple that had led the doggie massage were wearing sweaters with blinking lights. Three sisters wore matching elf sweater dresses. Even the animals in attendance wore outlandish sweaters.

Large Christmas lights the size of basketballs were hung from the ceiling. An oversize Christmas tree took up the far corner of the barn, the triangular top covered in a recycled sweater.

Standing at the edge of the crowd, taking it all in, Lucy added two jalapeño poppers to her plate. From the corner of her eye, she saw Hollie approach, her gentle features made softer in the glow of the twinkling lights. On Hollie's sweater, a poodle skated on an ice pond, a Santa hat slightly askew on its head.

Hollie hooked an arm with her. "Are you okay?"

"The party is amazing. Thanks for asking." And it was. She knew, objectively, this was a lovely gathering.

But her heart still felt heavy as she popped food in her mouth, trying her best to arrange her face toward levity as the flavors of melted cheese and spicy pepper mingled in her mouth.

Hollie shot her a pointed look. "That's not what I meant."

"Sorry to be in such a bah-humbug mood." She forced her grip on her plate to relax before she bent the thing in two. "This is just such a surreal holiday season. Riley was supposed to be getting married. And this is my first Christmas away from my son since he's with his dad."

"That has to be so hard. I'm sorry. George is a precious little boy."

"Thank you. I really do want to shake off this mood and join in the fun. Maybe I should have just stayed in the cabin." Except that would have meant being alone with Riley and the tension from that kiss when she still didn't know how she was feeling about that.

Should she ignore that it happened even though she was so very curious to explore those feelings?

Because he stirred her, more and more the longer they spent here away from their everyday world.

"You don't have to pretend to be happy. The Top Dog Dude Ranch is about authenticity. Healing. Sometimes, it's even just about surviving. There are plenty of other people here who have come at this time of year to distract themselves from the pain of loss."

In front of them, a line dance had formed around the base of the well-decorated oversize tree. A one-two step that she'd once danced to with Riley at prom.

Lucy looked around the room, from couples dancing to a family laughing together, and never would have guessed they were anything but full of joy. Were they like her, working to distract themselves by thinking of something, of anything, else?

Sighing, she admitted, "My mom struggled with depression, after she and my father split, especially during the holidays." She'd tried so hard to shield George from seeing her struggles.

"That had to be difficult for you."

"It was. It still is." While on one level it seemed odd to confide in this near stranger, Lucy also recognized a similar sadness in her, despite the trappings of happiness. She hated adding to the woman's burden. "Thank you for taking the time to talk to me. I know you must have a full plate tonight and with the other guests."

Lucy nodded toward the line dancers. Pairs in their ugly sweaters moved in time with the music. The women led backward by their partners toward the tree. They moved as a unit, a collective of Christmas colors on the dance floor.

Hollie brushed aside her concerns. "Everything here is running on autopilot by this point. They don't need me." Another hint of shadows chased through her eyes. "Our conversation is the first time I've felt free to let my guard down this whole week. Please, keep talking. What happened next with your parents?"

"Well, at one point, I went to live with my father for three months while Mom completed an intensive outpatient program. I couldn't see her very often. Twice the whole time. Dad said it was too far to drive. I think he assumed he was protecting me...or himself." She hadn't met Riley yet, didn't have his support.

Was she projecting some of her own feelings of rejection onto George? Maybe her own fears at being apart from her mother were making her all the more worried for her son, when there truly was a chance that Colin was offering him a better experience than the frightening one Lucy had. Colin was a shallow man, no question, but he really did adore George in his own way, and would do whatever he could to ensure their son had a nice holiday.

Smiling, Hollie tapped her temple. "It sounds to me like that even with their struggles, your parents managed to bring up an amazing daughter."

"That's kind of you." Unshed tears stung her eyes for a moment. The past weighed down on her present in ways that still sometimes took her by surprise. "I hope I didn't make you uncomfortable. It's definitely not a Christmassy cheer topic."

"We're all about authenticity, remember?" Hollie rubbed her shoulder.

"Some people seem to feel awkward when I bring up my mother's mental health. My ex-husband certainly did."

Colin had been nervous around her mother, like he was waiting for something bad to happen. She should have known her marriage was over the day she realized Colin was looking at her the same way. The expression on Colin's face sometimes had been so judgmental she'd told herself she had to have imagined it. That had been so much easier than acknowledging the truth in front of her.

"You deserved better than his lack of support for something so painful. I hope you know it." Hollie touched her arm lightly, squeezing. Her eyes knowing, as if she read Lucy's deepest thoughts, her insecurities. "Listen to me. My husband and I have not had a perfect marriage. There are days when I feel so very out of love. But there's respect and support between us, as there should be in a relationship."

Lucy bit her bottom lip, holding back the urge to tell Hollie that she just didn't know. That it was so easy to trust and be wrong. Except it would be rude to say to a near stranger—even one she found so easy to talk to. "Jacob seems to be a stand-up guy."

"He is. After I had a miscarriage, I suffered from postpartum depression. Even though our marriage was rocky, Jacob was there for me."

"I'm glad the two of you could pull together during a time of trouble. That's how marriage should work." She gave Hollie an impulsive hug. "Thank you for sharing that with me."

"I sense a kindred spirit in you." Hollie hugged her back before letting go. "Thank you for listening to me too."

"Of course." She hooked arms with the other woman. "Now come on, let's enjoy this incredible party."

"Absolutely. And be sure you and Riley take a spin on the dance floor during our signature Tennessee waltz."

And in spite of all of her intentions to keep her distance, physically, Lucy shivered in anticipation, every nerve alive at the prospect of being in Riley's arms.

Chapter Nine

Nearing midnight on Christmas Eve, the holiday hoedown was in full swing. Riley itched to change out of the ugly sweater, more than ready to see the end of this day. At least this had helped him to keep busy—to keep Lucy busy, as well. His gaze skimmed Lucy line dancing with Hollie and Nina. Christmases had been difficult in the past, and in spite of his plans, this one certainly wasn't a cakewalk.

The sound of George's cries still echoed in his head, like alcohol poured on the wound of his canceled wedding. All the twinkle lights above his head did nothing but remind Riley of the barn wedding Emily had planned. The same strands of Edison-style lights she'd been obsessed with for months.

His throat tightened for a second as his mind wandered from the conversation at hand. He'd done pretty well not thinking about Emily, surprisingly well, but it was hard to dodge all the reminders of what he'd planned.

And how poorly it had turned out. For him and for Lucy. For George too.

In front of him, one of the party's only guests under ten darted toward a plate of paw-shaped cookies, iced in green and red. Determined cowboy-boot steps pattered on the ground, reminding him of George. Anger rose and fell with each breath as he thought of Lucy's pain turned snowball fight earlier today.

Focus on the here and now. Weight shifting in his heels, he leaned forward, directing his attention back to the conversation at hand.

Standing beside a Christmas tree with a doghouse base for a stand, Riley listened to Jacob detail his latest horse purchase, while the waitstaff dressed in red-and-green-plaid shirts wove their way through the crowd carrying trays with cups of mulled cider.

Riley snagged a cup from the tray before the

young waiter with a lopsided Santa hat bustled away toward a laughing young family. "You're going to need a vacation of your own after all of this. As if holidays aren't exhausting enough."

"You'll be experiencing that for yourself next year once your horse-breeding ranch is up and running." Plate in hand, Jacob picked up a chicken wing.

"At least I won't be on the road." The words settled inside him, odd since he'd chosen to travel this year. What had made him want to stop running from home and its reminders of his father?

Suddenly the mulled cider lost its appeal and he set it aside. Heaviness seeped into his chest as the cup softly plunked down on the cocktail table that was draped in a red fabric with paw prints and candy canes. He knew the horse ranch was his future, but the dream palled since he would be experiencing it alone.

"You built quite a name for yourself on the rodeo circuit. What prompted you to decide to give it up now?" Jacob bit into the popper, setting the full plate next to his own glass mug of mulled cider.

"Tired of the bruises. Ready for roots." Who would have thought that decision would explode in his face?

His eyes wandered toward Lucy's spinning

body. Caught in the way she moved, her laughter full and unpretentious as she danced with Nina.

"That simple?"

Thumbing the sleeve of his red ugly sweater, he exhaled hard. "Buying a place of my own was always the plan eventually."

He'd only needed to move beyond ghosts of the past. He should have been better about communicating that to Emily. It would have saved him a boatload of heartache—not to mention giving up his apartment before his ranch was ready.

In fact, he probably should have realized how little he and Emily discussed anything of importance. Which made him flinch with guilt because it had always been so easy to talk about things that mattered with Lucy. Was it because they'd set aside their attraction in the beginning to focus on friendship? His gaze strayed to a couple of younger waitstaff members—a college-aged boy with curly brunette hair and a college-aged girl with honey-blond hair, exchanging a knowing look across the room. They were obviously smitten with one another. The girl's cheeks turned as scarlet as her red plaid shirt and Christmas hat.

The boy's eyes sparkled, never breaking eye contact with her even as he distributed mulled cider to three generations of men in the corner of the room. Once he and Lucy had a similar job in high school for a local animal rescue's gala. He remembered not being able to take his eyes off Lucy's easy manner with all the guests. She always carried a touch of kindness, even after all her hardship.

Jacob rocked back on his boot heels. "I'm sorry things didn't work out the way you wanted with your fiancée."

Scrubbing his hand over his head, Riley worked his jaw to relax the tension before he cracked a tooth. "It's for the best. It saved me from a divorce down the road. I've seen with Lucy how painful that is."

Through the gathering crowd on the dance floor, he caught sight of her with Hollie, and thought back to Lucy's red-rimmed eyes after Colin had walked out on her. The way she bore it all with grace in front of George.

"It's nice that Lucy can help you through this tough time. That kind of connection is special." Jacob smoothed a wrinkle on the tablecloth absently as an upbeat country tune pumped through the speakers.

Riley bristled, maybe because the comment came at a time he was still reeling from Emily's jealousy of Lucy. "There's never been anything romantic between us, though, if that's what you're hinting."

Although, that wasn't entirely true. Why was that underlying spark cropping up at every turn this week when he needed more than anything to tamp it down? Was it Emily's fault for putting it into his head in the first place?

"Not at all." Jacob held up a hand. "I apologize if my words indicated otherwise. You were clear on the phone that she's a good friend. Nothing more."

His unclenched his jaw, relaxing as his eyes darted back to the dance floor in time to see Lucy clapping her hands and catching his eyes. Electric awareness sparked in her green-valley gaze before she looked down at her dark brown leather boots.

Riley shook his head dismissively, drumming his fingers along the mug of mulled cider. Heat from the drink warmed his hand. "Even if I did have those kinds of feelings for her, Lucy's been burned." Badly. "I'm protective of her. Maybe that sounds convoluted...unfair to Emily and to Lucy."

"I'm the last one to give anybody advice on romance," Jacob said softly, wryly, lifting his mug for a swallow of cider.

"Clearly you know a thing or two to have a couple of decades of wedded bliss under your belt. Maybe it's the magic of this place." The scenery, the animals, the events all designed to ease tension, build connections. Except he currently felt anything but relaxed and connected.

And guessing from Lucy's dance-floor exit and move toward the coat check, she was feeling the same way.

What he'd give for holiday magic to make Lucy's smile spread wide across her pink lips and reach those eyes.

"Magic," Jacob said with a raised brow, "and a little bit of luck and a lot of hard work."

Just looking around at the holiday hoedown, the food, the decoration, made him tired. "Speaking of hard work, you've probably got a long evening ahead of you. I should let you get back to it."

"I enjoyed our chat." He clapped Riley on the back. "Congratulations again on your purchase. I look forward to buying horses for the Top Dog Dude Ranch from you one day."

"It would be an honor. Merry Christmas to you and your wife."

"To you and Lucy, as well."

His gaze shifted back to Lucy by the coat check, her face so forlorn he knew she was thinking about George. How could she not? This time last Christmas, Riley had been helping her put together a scooter for George from Santa.

He'd been so wrapped up in himself this evening, thinking about a wedding that didn't happen, a wedding that would have ended in disaster eventually, he'd lost sight of how he'd dodged a bullet. His pain? Was nothing compared to what Lucy was experiencing, an ongoing struggle.

Time to get his focus back on making this a holiday to remember for Lucy.

Lucy needed this late-night walk with Riley back to the cabin or she would never fall asleep. Her mind buzzed with the music, her body hyped from line dancing.

And the Tennessee waltz with Riley.

Plus, she'd sampled every food at the party. She knew that eating her feelings wasn't an emotionally healthy response, but she was all about surviving this night.

Sometimes survival looked a lot like carbs.

Still, no amount of jalapeños poppers could quell the turmoil inside her over spending the next week alone with Riley. Picking her way along the salted path, Lucy let the holiday carols wrap around her as she strolled past the living nativity under the stars. Two sheep and a cow clustered together, sheltering underneath the frame of the barn.

Boots crunched against the fresh dusting of

snow. No other footprints marked their way as she and Riley paused for a moment to look at the braying donkey who tossed its head in the hay-covered stall.

In another version of this night, Lucy would have followed her impulse to lean in toward Riley as the donkey continued its braying which echoed off trees in the valley. She would have said something funny. Made a rodeo joke. He would have playfully squeezed her hand in response, ribbing her about her fear of things with hooves.

But tonight, they were in new territory as they trudged on powdery snow, forging a path back to the cabin decked out in the soft glow of Christmas lights.

She searched for something benign to say, something that had nothing to do with sleeping under the same roof tonight. Alone. "Did Jacob have anything interesting to share about plans for the week? Or for your ranch?"

"We were just shooting the breeze about the horse ranch and how busy I'll be this time next year."

She nodded as she felt her mouth grow dry in the gust of cold air. *Say something* her internal voice screamed. Anything.

Instead, the wind shook snow off the trees

overhead, dusting the path. Her heart seized at the thought of how far away he would be living when he moved upstate, how different life would be for her and for George without Riley in the same apartment complex.

"Uh-huh." Brilliant. But better than crying about how much she would miss him.

"You and Hollie were sure deep in conversation earlier too. I hope you didn't feel like I'd abandoned you to a stranger when I was chatting with Jacob."

"Not at all. She's a delightful person, easy to talk to." She hugged herself, rubbing her arms even though her wool coat provided plenty of protection against the cold night air. "It's crazy how this time of year has us all sentimental about the good memories, but the bad ones too."

He slung an arm around her shoulder and tucked her against him. Just like old times. "I'm sorry. Today's been tougher than I imagined—"

"Because of Emily?" Guilt pinched that she'd given so little thought to his heartbreak today.

"Because of saying goodbye to George." His mouth went tight.

She melted against his side. "It tears me up and I can't even delude myself that it's not a big deal. I do know how he feels. My parents split so many times before they finally divorced. It was such a roller coaster—they hated each other and then they were in the glow of reunion, kind to each other, romantic. And my heart was still so raw. I thought that was the worst. Until they actually divorced and then it was nothing but bad. Even when they pretended to like each other, I sensed the truth."

"It must have been difficult, not having them talk to each other."

His voice was warm and comforting, caressing over her as they walked past a large family, laughing and singing on their way to their cabin.

And yet, how much comfort could his words bring when she hadn't been fully honest with him about her past where her parents were concerned?

"That's just what I told you because it was too embarrassing to share the truth. They did talk, horribly." Her boots crunched through the brittle ice, leaving shards as jagged as icy words. She'd never confided the painful truth to anyone else. "The fights were so bad they couldn't even go to each other's homes for the custodial handoffs. For a while we met in the parking lot of a fast-food restaurant. They would each try to make it better by buying me food in the drive-through but soon, even the smell of the food in the sack made me sick to my stomach. I always carried it to my room and threw it away."

And every time Colin drove away with her son crying in his car seat, Lucy felt the renewed weight of her failure to do better than her own parents.

"Oh man, Lucy," he said, stopping, cradling her shoulders in his hands, his face creasing with concern. "I thought we knew everything about each other, but you never told me all of that."

"Somebody needed to stay quiet," she answered, rolling her eyes. "I figured it might as well be me."

And yet now she could recognize the freeing power of speaking her truth, of sharing the hurts she'd kept hidden away. For all the faults of this day—and there were so, so many—she felt a little less burdened.

His fingers twitched along her shoulders, gripping in a near massage. Alluring in such a simple way. Her throat went dry, her heart fluttering in her chest.

Two deer—a doe and a buck—leaped from the tree line and into the path. She felt Riley's steady heartbeat quicken as the pair paused, wide chocolate eyes curious in the starlight.

Underneath pale moonlight, the doe quirked its slender head to the side in a posture that seemed assessing. Her mate, a muscled buck with tawny fur, rested his head atop her shoulders, echoing an embrace between lovers. His ears flicked forward.

The doe shuddered, taking a step forward before her mate followed into the dark, lovely brush.

Riley glanced down at her face, the heat of his breath igniting something deeper in this moment. Something intimate.

She cleared her throat, needing to break the tension. The taut awareness that hummed inside her. "Just to be clear, we're not going to sleep together tonight."

The words came out in a rush. Did they reveal how much she'd thought about the very thing she planned to deny them both?

"I don't recall asking," he said, the corners of his mouth twitching.

His easy comeback deflated the tension better than any rushed pronouncement of her own.

"Ouch," she said, chagrined. And, yes, grateful for his levity after a tense day. "Okay."

"Something has changed between the two of us." His brown eyes darkened, his face hazy through the cold puffs of breath between them. Still, he was Riley, so familiar, so strong and steady. "I know that, and I believe you do too."

"Yes, of course I do." Denying it would be fruitless. They understood each other too well.

Riley stepped closer, starlight at his back, ice glistening on the bare branches overhead. "Our friendship is the longest good relationship of my life. I don't want to risk it by being impulsive."

Toying with the zipper tab at the top of her coat, she eyed him, taking in his square jaw and broad shoulders. He was too handsome for his own good. "So, we're going to be careful? For each other?"

"I think we have to."

She agreed. And she trusted him. She also cared about him and knew tonight was too sad for either of them to spend alone. They'd resisted the attraction pretty well for nearly fifteen years. They could manage one more night. "I have a suggestion."

"Bring it on."

She gathered her courage and blurted before she could change her mind. "What if we shared the bed tonight? But no sex, no kissing. Just…not being alone on Christmas."

His arm under his head, Riley stared at the constellations visible through the bedroom skylight. It was a safer place to look than at his bedmate, his friend, his very beautiful friend—currently rocking flannel Christmas pj's.

Her cinnamon scent tempted his every breath.

Was it madness to tempt fate by sharing a bed with her tonight? Maybe. But he understood the impetus for the suggestion. He appreciated it, even, given the way his emotions had been tied in knots all day.

Talking to Lucy as he fell asleep might taunt the newfound awareness between them, but he needed his best friend tonight more than ever. After the hurt she'd felt this morning, Riley knew she needed him just as much.

He risked a sidelong glance at her. "This certainly beats the last time we shared a bed."

"It was memorable, to say the least," she said, lying on her side hugging a red checkered pillow stitched with a bright Santa Paws.

"It's one of my fondest memories."

She'd surprised him by showing up for the regional rodeo championship just after their senior year, driving three hours to see him compete. It was more than anyone had done for him before. The hotel had messed up her reservation. The town had been sold out because of the rodeo, so they'd shared a room. He'd planned to sleep on the floor, which she'd said was silly. She'd built a wall of pillows between them and they'd talked until nearly three in the morning.

The next day he'd placed second, even though he'd been slated to win. He'd been so tired he was lucky not to fall out of the saddle and get trampled.

He'd been embarrassed. But she'd cheered him

on and made him laugh, providing such a stark contrast to how his father would have reacted. His dad critiqued his every move in the saddle and in life to bits, making it clear all the ways Riley had fallen short of being the longed-for son. Riley didn't want to be that person who blamed things on his parents. He'd done his best to work hard and build a future.

It was hard not to beat himself up right now over what was clearly an epic failure with Emily. At Christmastime, no less.

Riley shifted his legs to make room for Pickles, who was pawing the edge of the mattress. The pup jumped up and curled into a tight ball at the foot of the bed, the brown fur a dark contrast to the pale rustic wood. "Christmases were tough, with Dad's drinking and drug use. But you knew that, right? Everyone knew."

"Yes, I did." She nodded, her hair in a red braid over her shoulder. "I figured you would talk about it when you were ready."

"Took me long enough." Seemed ridiculous, now, that he'd kept it to himself.

Pickles stretched, yawning while his paws pressed into Riley's legs causing him to inch ever so slightly toward Lucy and her cinnamon scent.

Devious little pup.

"As far as I'm concerned? Forcing someone to

talk about anything before they're ready is pretty fruitless."

"If only others ascribed to that same philosophy," he said wryly.

"Gossip hurts." Her voice was flavored with the pain of firsthand knowledge.

"Especially around the holidays."

Lucy toyed with the pine garland framing the oversize wooden headboard, fingers tracing absently on the edges of one of the snowflakes placed in the garland. "Seeing so many other people happy stings, that's for sure."

"Family joy is on overload everywhere you look. I'd thought I would replace those memories with a good one, having a holiday-season anniversary. Now I've just further wrecked future Christmases for myself."

She touched the back of his hand, sending a chill down his spine. "That first Christmas after my divorce was rough. I don't know how I would have made it through without you. I can never repay you for all you've done."

He'd shown up in a Santa costume with gifts, a full meal and plenty of spiked eggnog, determined to distract her. Tonight, the distraction came in a different form as they walked the line of friendship and something more.

Now that they'd discussed it—albeit briefly—he knew he'd be gnawing on the implications of the attraction day and night.

Riley sighed, his breath stirring the end of her braid. "You're here for me now, like you've been since high school. There's no score tab to keep. And I mean that." He catalogued this moment, took in the arch of her brows, the depths of green eyes, the faint smile on her pink lips. The past faded and he could only see the here, the now, with Lucy. "Merry Christmas, my friend."

"Right back at you." Her smile lit the room.

And sent a bolt of awareness pulsing through him.

There wasn't a pillow wall tall enough to keep him from wanting her.

Chapter Ten

Standing at the kitchen counter, Lucy put the finishing touches on breakfast, with her tablet propped on the counter for a conversation with George. She couldn't get enough of his precious face and dear voice. It felt like longer than a day since he'd left.

His bright blue eyes showed no signs of the sadness from the day before as he moved through Colin's house. Christmas classics crooned in the background, the volume almost low enough that Lucy had trouble making out the lyrics of a jazzy "Jingle Bells."

"Santa Claus brought me so many toys." He turned the camera toward a towering Christmas tree encircled with white lights and perfectly matching orb and spire ornaments. The thirteen-foot wall-to-ceiling windows framed the tree and cast morning light on a pile of toys—a new bike, stuffed animals, Lego sets. "Riley was right."

"About what, sweetie?" She pulled her cranberry scones from the oven and tried not to think about how last year she'd made George pancakes shaped like a snowman.

"Santa knew where to find me." George flipped the camera back as he maneuvered to the elegant farmhouse coffee table in front of the mantel. He held up a porcelain plate with a reindeer and text that read Cookies for Santa. Crumbs tumbled to the perfectly plush carpet.

"Of course Santa knew." She set the tray of scones beside a quiche. The warm scents of Christmas morning did little to lift her mood.

He brushed a cascade of curls from his narrowing eyes. "Did he bring anything for Pickles?"

Nodding, she leaned her elbows on the cool countertop. "A new bed, a chew bone and a stuffed giraffe."

From the other end of the connection, George whirred around the corner of a white linen sofa. Joy lit his movements as she watched him enjoy his morning.

A pang of sadness gripped her heart. Everything was perfect for her son. Except she missed being a part of this memory. A lump threatened the back of her throat. Instead, she plastered a smile on her face.

George jumped with his tablet, spinning around while his big toothed grin widened. "Oh, I bet Pickles loves that. Old Giraffey was his favorite. Except he tore old Giraffey up. It makes me sad when I break my toys. Do you think Pickles was sad?"

Someone must have eaten a lot of sugar for breakfast. "I think Pickles is happy now. He's out for a walk with Riley now. Do you want to see?"

Turning her tablet, she walked fast to the window and pointed the camera toward the front lawn. Pickles pranced in the snow, digging, coming back up with the scarf from their snowman.

"Aww," George crooned. "That's cute. Here's Ace."

He turned the phone to show a chocolate Labrador sleeping in front of the tree. Calm and collected on the oversize white tiles, the lab didn't even open a lazy eye at all the commotion.

"Ace is a handsome dog." She couldn't fault the pup's behavior. Not that she wanted the dog to be naughty, but did Colin's life have to be so very perfect?

"We took him for a walk in the snow this morning." He turned the phone back to his face—well, showing half of his face as the phone wobbled. "Did you remember to walk Pickles after I left yesterday?"

"Sure did. After dinner last night," at the ugly sweater party, "we took Pickles for a walk. They had the nativity petting zoo set up again under the stars last night. People gathered and sang songs."

She and Riley had done a careful dance this morning after sharing the bed last night, intimate in its own way, even in a king-size space as big as a barge.

As if conjured by her thoughts, Riley opened the cabin door, an icy gust of morning air sweeping in with him. Pickles sprinted inside, leash trailing him on his way to the water bowl.

"Merry Christmas, Riley," George called, waving hard and fast on the screen. "Merry Christmas, Mommy." He kissed the screen. "I gotta go open more presents. Love you. Bye."

"Love you too," she rushed to say but the call had already disconnected.

She felt like crying her eyes out. Every breath came faster, threatening hyperventilation. All of the weight of separation crashed down on her.

Footfalls sounded behind her just before she felt

a warm hand cup her shoulder, squeeze, stay, comforting. No words. Thank goodness, because she probably would have broken down in sobs and the last thing she wanted was to weight down the room with her own sadness.

Lucy blinked once. Twice. Willed the tears in her eyes to stay put as she glanced up at Riley. "I'm okay. Really. He's having a good time. That's what matters most."

"I know he misses you." His deep brown eyes held her in another embrace, one built on years of understanding and trust.

Nodding, she couldn't talk more on that subject without breaking down. "Do you want to exchange gifts now?"

"You're so sad," he said, brushing back a strand of her hair, "as am I. So, I'd rather wait, if that's alright with you. Let's stretch the day out."

"Of course. It will give me some time to put distance between myself and that phone call." Her chin quivered. "I just miss my little boy so much."

He hauled her in for a quick, hard hug, then stepped back with that understanding way of his, as if he knew she was still on edge. "That breakfast smells amazing. Let's eat up. And after that, I know just what you need."

"You do?"

"You need to get back in the saddle."

Riley's gloved hands ran down the side of the cognac leather saddle, moving on instinct to the girth. Foxtrot, a stout buckskin, let out a huff as Riley tightened the girth outside the large, top-of-the-line horse barn. The skies were clear blue with a bright winter sun.

For this time of year, the conditions didn't get much better.

He patted the gelding's neck as he investigated the running martingale and the bridle. His heart hammered, as he checked and double-checked every strap and buckle, every potential place where tack could fail, because he wanted this outing to be a success for Lucy. In a perfect world, he would be taking this ride with both Lucy and George.

But the most important thing right now? Helping keep her mind occupied. He just hoped this didn't backfire with her landing in the snow.

Lucy's leather-gloved fingers toyed with the end of her ponytail. Her stonewashed jeans were mostly covered by a pair of tan suede chaps to help her grip the saddle better and keep her seat. The puffy Top Dog Dude Ranch jacket was zipped to her neck, but still managed to show her curves.

A half smile that revealed her nerves quirked across her face, pitch rising as she spoke. "As if riding a horse in the summer isn't scary enough? You want me to ride in the snow."

"Have I ever let anything bad happen to you?" Other than not speaking up about his reservations about Colin? He stifled a wince.

She pushed snow around with her riding boots, tension easing at least a hint from her green eyes. "You've always been there for me."

"Good. Just keep reminding yourself of that." He appreciated her faith in him. It had sure seen him through tough times of his own. "Let's get this show on the road."

She pressed a hand to her stomach in a way she often did when nervous. "Alright then, it's now or never."

In three quick steps, Lucy moved toward the buckskin. Determination set in her jaw as Riley gave her a leg up. He was all too aware of the ways their bodies touched as she mounted the horse. Giving himself time to regain objectivity, he spent a few moments adjusting her stirrups and helping her find her grip on the braided leather reins. She settled into the saddle and he watched her for a moment. Checking. Assessing her comfort level for nerves.

"Everything alright? We can stop any time."

"All's well. Thank you for asking, though. I promise to keep you posted if I'm approaching a freak-out." She stroked Foxtrot's neck. The gelding's ears perked forward, ready and attentive.

He untied his own horse, Trickster, a pretty liver chestnut horse with tall white stockings on all four legs, from the nearby hitching post. In a fluid motion as natural as drawing breath, he mounted Trickster and applied gentle calf pressure to bring his horse next to Lucy and Foxtrot.

Clicking his tongue, he snagged Foxtrot's attention. The horse took a lazy step forward, hoof crunching into the snow that gathered along the fence line.

While Lucy had made breakfast, he'd studied the trails from the information packet in Lucy's binder. He'd picked the kid-friendly looping path that meandered through the main part of the ranch. Even in the snow, the terrain promised to be easy and the ride short.

It offered a perfect reintroduction for Lucy into the world for riding.

She held the reins loosely, just as Riley had showed her. Her concentration present in the slightly furrowed brow.

For all of her hesitation about horses, she

seemed like she belonged in the saddle. Her calm stillness, despite whatever was going through her mind, ensured her mount didn't feel any agitation.

She nodded toward the ranch's commons area. "Did you see the list of activities they have going on? All sorts of things for fun and team building."

"Such as?" he asked, hoping that if she kept talking, it would take her mind off the ride, that she would feel more at ease.

Keeping Trickster's pace slow and even, he hoped that having his horse calm and collected would help Lucy and Foxtrot as they made their way down the fence line toward the outdoor ice-skating rink. Even from this distance, Riley noted a family with Santa hats and reindeer-antler headbands swirl around the ice. He tucked that detail away, making a mental note to stay vigilant in his watch of Lucy as they approached movement.

While Jacob had said Foxtrot was calm, he wanted to stay aware of any potential places a horse might spook. He turned his focus back to Lucy as she spoke, nerves easing from her voice as she described the upcoming activity.

"Well," she said, "the brochure listed an ice-breaker session where they gather a room full of people, then they randomly assign animal sounds.

You make yours and try to find the other person making the same noise."

She was more beautiful than even the majestic landscape. Sleeping with her last night had been… surreal. He'd been surprised by her overt discussion of *no sex* even as she suggested sharing a bed. The notion still circled around in his brain. The draw was real, but knowing how stressed she was about her son helped him resist—even though he would have preferred to distract them both in the best way possible.

Just the thought threatened to lure him in. He shifted his focus back to the landscape around him. Snowcapped mountain peaks rose in the distance; a forest of skinny leafless trees rustled in the wind.

He watched her shoulders relax ever so slightly as they moved beyond the rink toward the main lodge where a couple who had been line dancing the night before loaded suitcases and presents into the cab of a lifted green pickup truck. Another couple hoisted skis onto the top of a dark blue SUV.

Adjusting his black Stetson, he couldn't hold back a smile as he imagined the icebreaker Lucy described. "Sounds silly, but would certainly loosen up a crowd. What else?"

Her gaze shifted from the saddle horn to his

face, another sign of ease and comfort that set his heart galloping with relief.

She looked skyward for a moment, thinking as sunlight illuminated her porcelain skin. "There's a 'protect the egg' game to encourage teamwork. Another game where they give out puzzle pieces and you find your match."

The path veered slightly to the left, putting the living nativity scene off in the distance to their right. Trickster and Foxtrot plodded lazily through the snow, pace unhurried and unbothered even as the donkey brayed. What a chatty beast.

"We would excel at that. It would almost be unfair to the other couples." Couples? The word stopped him up short. He pushed words through though before she could notice the quiet—and that she was still on a horse. "What else?"

As they navigated downhill, more cabins came into focus, dotting the incline with pockets of Christmas-morning activity. Young children darted across lawns, and peals of laughter floated on the wind as they continued their descent.

"There's a whole afternoon series of workshops focused on making things for the local shelter they support. Crafting dog beds and toys, building climbing towers for cats."

"I saw something about using wool from the sheep to make blankets."

"You would be into that?" she asked, surprise in her voice.

"Nah." He chuckled. "But it sounded cool."

"You're trying to keep me occupied talking so I won't notice I'm riding a horse."

He steered them toward the close of the loop, past the cabin where the Archers were staying. Nina, Douglas and their twin girls had sleds in their hands.

"Busted. But you have to admit, you're really riding well."

"You're the one doing all the work." She rested her hand on the horn, shoulders moving with the buckskin's smooth gait.

"But you're doing hanging in there with style."

Lucy tossed her head back, red hair from her ponytail wind-caught as her body shook with laughter. The sound lit a fire within him. Her carefree, real laugh gave her a glow as the peaks of the stable came into view.

"See," he said, gesturing to the approaching end of the trail, "that wasn't bad at all. You'll be taking fences and barrel racing before you know it."

"I doubt that, but I can see myself riding again, as long as you keep it easy like today." She glanced sidelong at him. "I want to be a part of your world too. You've been so kind and generous helping me build the dog-walking clientele."

Trickster's ears perked up as the stable drew closer. Energy seemed to move through the Thoroughbred as he recognized his home. "I've had fun honing my skills on dog behavior."

Riley pointed toward the post where they'd started, and Lucy nodded, guiding her horse with new confidence. And if he were being honest, the sight made it into the top three moments of this trip.

They brought their horses to a halt, and Riley slid down first and tied his horse to the post with a quick-release knot.

Lucy said, "Maybe we can take a day trip up to see the land you bought. All the pictures were taken before this big snow."

Thinking about the property was a dicey subject now that he was going to be a bachelor. Alone. Was that why it felt so right to visit the subject with Lucy?

No. It would have been great to have her there regardless. She and George were integral parts of his life, of every decision he made for the future.

"That would be a great way to ring in the New Year." He reached up for her. "Thanks."

Riley pointed to the horn, reminding her to put

her weight into her hands as she swung her right leg up and over Foxtrot's hindquarters.

"Steady," he warned, cupping her waist as he eased her down. "Wouldn't want you falling the second your feet are on the ground again."

Her hands stayed on his shoulders, her green eyes serious, concerned. "Riley, I'm really sorry about Emily. In many ways, she seemed right for you, with her love for horses and riding."

Too bad Emily's proclaimed love for horses had been more about the stars riding than the sport itself. But the last thing he wanted was to discuss an ex who, for the life of him right now, he couldn't recall why he wanted to marry in the first place. He certainly couldn't imagine Emily making the same sort of selfless choices that Lucy made on a regular basis without asking anything in return.

A Top Dog Dude Ranch staff member emerged from the mouth of the barn, before untying Trickster and taking Foxtrot's reins. He led the pair into the barn for a proper grooming.

Riley nudged Lucy with his elbow, head quirking to the walking trail that would lead them from the stables to their cabin. Bright sun illuminated their stroll to their temporary home. Cabins on the path were still lit with Christmas lights, and white smoke from chimneys added a sense of clouds to the clear-sky day.

An easy silence fell over them as boots pressed snow. Maybe the first easy silence since this trip had started, and for that he was grateful.

For Riley, horses were a space where everything felt possible. And while he didn't fault Lucy for being horse shy after her tumble all those years ago, he was grateful that he could share a bit of that world with her today.

As their cabin came into view, Riley cleared his throat, breaking the silence. "Thank you for going riding today. I hope I didn't push too hard on getting back in the saddle. I know horses aren't your thing."

Her green eyes flicked from him to the frozen patch on the path ahead. She stepped around the ice on the ground, maneuvering ever so slightly toward him.

"My interest in your world is real. I would have asked more about your new place, earlier, but I didn't want to interfere with plans you had with Emily. I already feel like I quiz you too much and take up too much of your time with George and projects around the apartment—"

"You haven't done anything wrong." He took her hand in his as they walked, her warmth radiating through the mittens. "I have offered because I want to be a part of your life and George's. Just as you're a part of my life."

They stopped walking, lingering beneath the limbs of the Christmas tree and near the remnants of Frosty.

"It was easier to stay friends when I was with Colin. And you were with Emily." She tipped her face up to his, her gaze filled with all the desire they'd worked so hard to deny. "And there wasn't…"

"This." He dipped his head to hers, his mouth covering hers.

The rightness of the connection flooded him so completely he couldn't call to mind why he'd denied it. His hands slid up her arms, his fingers gripping her, aching for her in a way that went beyond anything he'd known. No longer denying the feeling gave him…freedom. Freedom for more.

Although that "more" wasn't feasible out here. Now. And while he was certain of what he wanted, he had to make sure she felt the same.

"It's definitely more complicated now. What if 'this' destroys our friendship?" Her breath filled the air with faster puffs of white as they stood outside their cabin. "Because I don't know what I would do without you in my life."

He agreed. Every landmark moment, he'd discussed with her first. He didn't know how he would sift through decisions without her to brainstorm with.

But he also knew that if they continued on as they were, their friendship would fracture under the strain of the newfound chemistry.

Newfound?

Okay, it had always been there, but now, it could no longer be suppressed, denied or written off as a passing attraction. "Lucy, ignoring the attraction certainly hasn't worked. It's time to approach this head-on."

Taking a step back, he waited. The next move had to be hers.

The next move was hers.

Standing at the foot of the cabin steps with Pickles pawing the window inside, Lucy understood that she needed to choose her next move before much longer. The way Riley gave her space to decide was one of the many things she appreciated about him. But she also needed to make up her mind soon or her feet were going to freeze in spite of her fuzzy boots and two pairs of socks—if she wasn't buried in snow first.

Still, concerns lined up in Lucy's mind one after

the other as she stared from Riley to the cabin door. And back at her quietly brooding friend again. A sharp inhale of winter air bit against her lungs, sending her thoughts into overdrive.

Would this wreck their relationship?

What if he regretted the decision and she was left embarrassed?

How would they get through the rest of the retreat if sex made things awkward between them?

Why hadn't she worn lacy underwear?

One thing, though, she knew for certain. She was tired of saying no. Weary with worrying. She—they—needed an escape from all that the world had dumped onto them. Whether the problems stemmed from their own poor choices or just bad luck, she was done trying to figure it all out. She needed to escape from weighty thoughts and just feel.

Was it risky to take him up on the offer steaming from his brown eyes? Yes. Might she regret it the second the sweat cooled on their sated bodies? Possibly.

But as Riley had said, ignoring, pushing back the feelings and just hoping they would go away hadn't worked for them—at all. She'd been afraid of riding a horse and that had turned out better than expected—had even been fun.

Maybe she had been overthinking things. Regardless, it was time to try the only thing left.

She was going to check out those benefits with her best friend.

Chapter Eleven

Riley was so relieved he almost melted into the snow.

But now that Lucy was finally stepping into his arms, he didn't intend to waste a single second.

Banding an arm around Lucy's waist, Riley anchored her to him as they kissed their way up the cabin steps, careful not to slip on the ice. The world was unsteady for more reasons than a little snow along the planks.

The soft give of her lips against his, the press of her body, made him want her even more. She felt perfect against him, every curve fitting to him, her hips swaying against him in a way that revved him hotter. He broke contact only long enough to tap out the code on the security pad, then drew her to him again and backed her inside. He kicked the door closed again.

Sealing them alone together in the cabin.

A flip of the remote ignited the flames in the fireplace. The tree lights twinkled from the corner, two gifts wrapped and waiting.

For later.

Right now, he had one thing on his mind. Unwrapping *her*. The best present ever and the only gift he wanted.

She purred her appreciation, and he agreed. He soared his Stetson onto the table as she tugged off her hat. Coats, scarves and gloves landed in a trail on the floor.

Her hair carried the scent of the crisp fresh air, pine and cedar, reminiscent of their ride. The brave way she'd tackled riding a horse, facing her fears, humbled him. She always had been the boldest person he'd ever known—in all the best ways.

And right now, she was beautifully embracing her bold side, one button at a time on her turquoise flannel shirt, revealing a peek of her white satin bra. He mirrored her movements, parting his own shirt. Her jeans gone, then his. Their underwear wasn't any more revealing than their bathing suits and they'd been swimming together more times than he could recall.

This?

This, though, was different. Her matching white panties and bra called to him, her gaze lingering on his plaid boxers.

"Are you sure? About you and I together?" He gestured back and forth, aching to close the distance between them, but willing to wait. He couldn't mess up this moment. "I need to hear you say it."

Reaching, she stroked a finger down his arm. "I am absolutely certain I want to sleep with you."

She linked hands with him, palm warming him more than the fire to his bare back. "Make love with you."

She stepped closer, her breasts skimming his chest. "And explore this chemistry that's been such a challenge to us both since high school."

"So," he said, resting his forehead against hers, "is that a yes?"

"Yes, yes and yes," she repeated, cupping his face in her hands and arching up on her toes for another kiss. The sweep of her tongue carrying the sweet hint of cider and *her*.

He'd known the attraction was strong, but he'd had no idea. And from the passion in her touch and surprise in her eyes, he could sense this was a revelation for her, as well.

"The bedroom?" he asked between breathless gasps.

"How about here?" She gestured toward the Christmas tree and glowing hearth. "In front of the fire."

"Perfection. Like you." He tugged her deeper into the room.

"Sweetly said, but can we stop talking now?" She backed a step with him, hooking a finger in the waistband of his boxers and releasing with a snap. Her eyes vixen green.

"Yes, ma'am. Talking is over…" Grinning, he closed the distance between them, drawing her to him. The feel of her smooth flesh against his skin was bliss. "Unless it's to tell you how absolutely beautiful you are."

Flames flickered in the fireplace, flicking higher, casting the room—her—in a warm glow. Her red hair alight with honey tones. Light and shadow played across her body, the length of her legs, the dip of her waist, the curve of her breasts.

Desire surged through him, heat, for her. For Lucy.

But he also needed to protect her. "I don't want

to put a damper on things, but we need birth control. I didn't bring anything."

She froze for a moment, her forehead furrowing. Panic set in as he realized she wouldn't have expected this any more than he had. He did the math on how far he would have to drive to find birth control. Not very festive.

Lucy's face cleared and she clasped her hands together. "Condoms. In the bedroom, bedside table, along with some other welcome toiletries. Apparently, the ranch takes responsible sex very seriously." She held up a hand. "Don't move. I'll be right back."

He watched the twitch of her hips in white satin as she made fast tracks to the bedroom, humming the whole way. She managed the best balance of cute, funny, sexy all in one amazing package.

He spread a quilt decorated with deep red poinsettias on the floor in front of the fireplace, lights from the tree illuminating the room as dusk chased away the day.

She tucked her head around the doorjamb, condom in her fingertips. Her nose scrunched adorably as she hesitated. "Is it awkward that we're using birth control that was meant for your honeymoon?"

Somehow using the condoms this way felt right.

Destined. He had zero thought for the alternative. "I'm not worried if you aren't."

She stepped toward him, apparently reassured. The heat was back in her eyes, her attention fixed on him. "The only thing I'm worried about right now is how much longer it will be until we can finally, finally be together."

"I couldn't agree more." He plucked the condom from her hand and hauled her close.

Placing the packet on the sofa, he reclined her onto the quilt, kneeling beside her, then stretching out beside her. He'd wondered about a moment like this more than he cared to admit, and he didn't intend to squander a second. He angled his mouth over hers, cradling her hip in his hand, rocking her against him.

Her sighs of excitement grew, her hands gripping at his arms, her fingers digging in as she swung her leg over his. She stroked the arch of her foot along his calf. Every brush and nip a sweet temptation.

Then her touch grew urgent, and the last scraps of underwear were swept and kicked away leaving them bare against each other. Finally. The press of her breasts against his chest sent desire surging through his veins.

But he had so much more of her he wanted to experience, explore, his hand learning each inch of her. Determined to bring her as much pleasure as her touch brought him.

She nipped his ear and whispered, "We have all night—all week even. We can go slower later. Right now, I want… I want…"

"Me too," he growled against her neck, grasping for the condom.

She snatched the packet from him and sheathed him in a delicious stroke before he stretched out on top of her. Slowly, he pressed into her, the warmth of her threatening to send him over the edge. He paused. Waiting. Trying to regain control.

Their gazes held. He read in her eyes what he knew she must see in his. This moment, their first connected, the intimacy all the more intense because of their history. They already knew one another so well. And now this…

Then he couldn't form any more thoughts. He lost himself in sensation. In Lucy. The hint of cinnamon in her perfume. The creamy softness of her skin and husky music of her warm sighs against his neck.

There was a synergy in their lovemaking born of their friendship. No awkwardness or search for matching rhythm, in synch on when to speed up, slow down with each thrust. Until the urge to finish hummed through him, his pulse pounding in his ears. He held back, waiting for her, watching for signs that she was...

Her head pressed into the quilt, her throat a beautiful arch. Seeing the flush spread across her chest, hearing her sighs, he let himself follow her over the cliff of completion. Burying his face against her shoulder, he let his hoarse shout flow against her skin, wave after wave of sensation rippling through.

With a final shudder, he rolled to his back and tucked her to his side. Silence echoed through the cabin, broken only by the crackle of the flames and sleepy breaths from Pickles.

His thoughts were a scrambled mess and he didn't know how long it would take to find his footing again. One thought, though, shone through.

They may have a perfect synergy in bed, but when it came to life? They were masters at getting the timing all wrong. If he didn't want to mess up tonight's tenuous connection, he needed to proceed with caution. It had always been too easy to think of them as a family.

And they both knew the pain of having that dream of having a family taken away.

Sleep tugged at Lucy, not surprising since she'd just labored for a full day to give birth. Thank goodness she hadn't been alone. Given that Colin had been away on a business trip and hadn't been able to make it back in time, Riley had to step in as her coach: She didn't know how she would have made it through the experience without the support of her best friend.

And now, having someone to share the wonder of time with her new baby.

Overhead lights hummed quietly as her gaze caught on the features of her newborn. The fact her baby was in the world sent waves of love coursing through her as she stared at her son's face, memorizing his features. A whisper of red hair on his head. Peace in the shape of his Cupid's bow little mouth.

Pressing a hand to her chest, she briefly tore her eyes from the newborn in her arms, looking from the hospital bed to the gray chair to the left of her bed, next to the window that let sunbeams dance across the faux wood floor. Riley's elbow pressed into the chair's arm, cradling his head and hiding his eyes from her view.

"Riley?" she whispered softly in case he was asleep. Then smiled when he straightened, his arms stretching while his muscles strained against the surgical scrubs he'd donned for the delivery. He'd been amazing. A rock during the hours of pain and

anxiety. "Thank you for being there for me. This went far and above friendship duties."

Scrubbing a hand over his face, he pushed out of the chair and walked to her bedside, stopping by the arrangement he'd brought—white roses and blue amaryllis, her favorites. "Being on call when you needed me was absolutely smack-dab in the friendship playlist."

"I imagine if you were my gal pal maybe." Laughing, she cradled her son closer, rocking him gently in her arms.

"Well, that's sexist, right, George?" Riley tapped a finger on the infant's nose, then looked up at Lucy again. "You are still naming him George, aren't you?"

His hand lingered on the white herringbone blanket as he searched her face.

"Yes, that's the plan." Unless Colin had changed his mind. They'd only been able to speak via Face-Time for a few minutes after George was born. Colin had said he was rushing to the airport to catch a hop. She tamped down disappointment that he'd missed out, but reminded herself that having her healthy son was what mattered most.

"Thank goodness the name's a keeper, because I have a passel of personalized gifts just waiting for him in my truck." He winked. "I should prob-

ably wait until after you've been discharged. I've been buying since you told me you were expecting, so there's a lot of gear."

"You're so sweet to shower him with so much." She held his warm gaze, thankful for the way he was always there at important times in her life.

"Nothing but the best rodeo gear to get my little godson started out right."

"I'll be sure to take tons of photos and send them to you while you're on the road." She would miss him.

"And we can FaceTime so he won't be scared when I come for visits—"

A knock on the door drew Lucy's and Riley's attention. George stirred slightly, his eyes blinking open as a nurse in pastel-colored dinosaur scrubs crossed the threshold. Her warm brown skin and rosy smile set Lucy at ease.

"It's time to check your vitals, Momma." The nurse's singsong voice filled the hospital room with even more brightness. Somehow making this moment more real for Lucy.

Riley squeezed her hand, offering a beaming closed-mouth smile. Lucy squeezed back as the nurse checked her temperature and recorded the number into her digital tablet.

"I'm happy to report so far, so good." She

wrapped the blood pressure monitor around Lucy's arm while Riley took George. Her son continued to sleep soundly, nestled against her best friend's chest.

The machine tightened on Lucy's arm before releasing the pressure with a long hiss. The nurse recorded the information, removing the blood pressure unit before adding, "Look at the three of you. It warms my heart to see such a cute family, and one that is so in tune to each other's needs."

Lucy's heart lurched and she fought back tears, avoiding Riley's gaze.

The nurse patted her on the hand. "Try to get some rest when you can. I'll be back in to check on you."

Riley handed George back to Lucy. She pressed her son to her chest which still felt heavy. Tears still threatened to fall and she didn't trust her voice to be steady yet.

The nurse left the room which had grown too silent and too loud all at once.

Riley let out a little bark of laughter, scrubbing the back of his neck. "Well, that was a little awkward."

Lucy nodded, gathering her nerves. She swallowed, her mouth tense as words leaped from her *lips. "Colin texted that he was on his way. You can go. I'm fine and you must be exhausted."*

"You can't get rid of me that easily. I'm staying until he arrives."

Riley brushed some of the hair that'd fallen from her bun back behind her ear. The same way he'd done when they were in high school with all the world and its promise ahead of them. Their eyes locked, a silent understanding of how deep their friendship went enlivening each breath.

A familiar masculine voice sounded from the doorway. Colin. "Well, I'm here now." He stepped inside, red roses in hand. His icy blue eyes narrowed at Riley. "Thanks for the help but you can go now so I can meet my son..."

Lucy pushed through the fog of sleep, curled against Riley's side in bed, stars twinkling through the skylight, only a few hours left on Christmas Day.

Soft sheets caressed her. Her legs tangled with his, and the moon provided enough dim glow she could see the throw pillows discarded in the corner of the room.

Her hand clenched on his bare chest over his heartbeat, trying to anchor herself in the now. While the day George had been born was a blessing, it was tough not to remember that time and recall where Colin had really been—or rather who he'd been with. She hadn't known the truth until two years later.

But once his betrayal was revealed by his disgruntled ex-girlfriend on the side, Lucy found it impossible to look at the past in the same way again.

Turning her head on the pillow, she studied Riley's sleeping profile. A man of strength. Of honor. She'd thought the day George was born that she couldn't be any closer to her friend. But today? Making love with Riley? She still couldn't wrap her mind around what had been the best sex of her life.

With her best friend.

She'd thought things were complicated between them before. But now? She couldn't go back to the way things were in the past. Being with Riley today had only whetted her appetite for more of him. If one time together produced this much emotion, how much more would it compound with time?

But what if he didn't feel the same?

She didn't know how she could survive that kind of loss in her life. So where did that leave her?

Scared.

Afraid of being hurt in a way that far exceeded even the wreckage Colin had bought to her life.

Going forward, she needed to proceed cautiously. No launching into things headfirst. She needed to take a step back and approach her next move in an organized fashion.

Time to create a new binder.

"Oh my goodness," Lucy exclaimed, peering into the gift box. "These binders are gorgeous."

Sitting with Lucy at the base of the tree, Riley couldn't help but wonder now if the present was too bland. But when he'd gone Christmas shopping for Lucy, he hadn't been thinking of them having hot sex.

And yet, here they were. Half-dressed. Her in his national championship T-shirt and him in Christmas plaid sleep pants, the remains of their turkey dinner on the hearth. They'd ordered the ranch's meal delivery, uninterested in leaving the cabin, preferring instead to make good use of the bed in the best of ways.

He pulled his attention back on to the moment at hand. "I saved the receipt if you want to exchange anything."

Reverently, she placed her hand on the mint-colored leather binder, a smile spreading across her face in the firelight and soft glow of the Christmas lights.

"It's perfect. You know me so well." She dug

through the box, taking her time with each layer. A small pile of tissue paper formed to her side. "And all of the tabs and labeling accents. This is so much nicer than anything I could afford." She angled forward to kiss him, lingering in a way that was familiar and new all at once. "Thank you."

The kissing was a definite benefit of what they'd shared. He could handle being thanked that way all the time.

"You're welcome." He slid his hand to cup the back of her neck, his fingers testing the texture of her wavy hair. How could he have not known how soft the locks were? He'd touched her… He just hadn't *touched* her.

She smiled against his mouth, then rocked back to sit, her green eyes reflecting the lights on the tree. "Did you see me eyeing them when we were out shopping for George's birthday party?"

"I may have noticed." He'd had to concoct a distraction so he could slip back to the aisle and take photos of the items she'd admired so he could purchase them later. "Although to be fair, I can't imagine how you could be any more organized."

She crinkled her nose. "Thank you?"

As he had done countless times before, he reached for her slender hands and gave them a squeeze. But tonight, the touch sent an awareness of their connection through him. "You know that I think you're incredible."

"Your confidence in me has carried me through some of the toughest times. Like the day George was born." She touched her chest for a moment before the smile returned to her eyes. "Okay, enough of that. Open your gift."

He tugged the plaid bow off and peeled back the red paper to find... Business cards for his horse farm. "Wow, that's so thoughtful."

Cradling the box in his hand, he looked at the well-designed typeset, a logo that was exactly what he'd imagined but would never have known how to execute. Even after all these years, Lucy's eye for style and her ability to pull fonts, patterns and images together into something so aesthetically pleasing never ceased to amaze him.

"I hope it wasn't presumptuous of me," she said nervously, chewing the inside of her lip. "Maybe you would have preferred to design them yourself."

"They're perfect. You know I would have been knocking on your door for advice anyway. Thank you."

Lucy wrapped her arms around herself and looked at him for a long moment. In a quieter voice, she continued, "We're going to miss having you right down the apartment hallway, seeing you whenever we want."

Her smile thinned. The same look that had been on her face when he'd announced he was leaving town—and her—to pursue a career on the rodeo circuit. Supportive, but tinged with sadness.

A void opened up inside him, one of loneliness that went beyond anything he'd felt hitting the road before. In the past, he'd always known he would be returning to Lucy. Now? He was putting down roots. Seeing Lucy would be compartmentalized to weekend vacations.

Already, he could see those trips growing shorter, further apart. Nonexistent.

An unacceptable outcome.

He didn't need to ponder one instant longer on the next step. "You and George should move to my ranch."

Chapter Twelve

Move to his ranch?

The words pinballed around inside Lucy's brain, stirring anxiety with every ricochet. Fingertips working into the thick fabric of the quilt. Trying to find purchase. Some kind of anchor while the world spun out from under her. And although they still sat at the base of the tree with presents in their laps, she had the sudden sensation of feeling far-away from this moment and this place.

She toyed with the clip on the binder. "What do you mean?"

"Just what I said." He lifted her hands and

clasped them in his. "You and George could relocate to my farm."

"I have an apartment." She shivered, and knew it had nothing to do with the fact she was only wearing Riley's T-shirt. "And I have a business."

The fire roared to her side, illuminating a whole new path before her eyes. Her best friend's warm brown eyes lit from something more than just the flames in the hearth as he cocked his head to the side.

"That's the beauty of dog walking." He pushed aside her new binders and drew her to his side, his arm a warm weight around her shoulders. "You can start that up in a new location. Or you could apply for openings at vet clinics."

Her head was spinning. He was moving too fast, leaving little time to adjust to this new dynamic. Why couldn't they just enjoy the moment? They had a pocket of time away from the world here at the ranch before they had to worry about the big picture. Riley wasn't normally this impulsive, and that worried her. It wasn't in keeping with what she expected from her grounded, steady friend.

"Or I could continue my life as it is." Except it wouldn't be the same. Riley was moving. And while he'd traveled before, this was different.

Permanent. She shivered again.

Her hand wandered off the edge of the quilt. Never before had she wished to put Riley in a binder to make sense of him before now. To make sense of them.

She knew him better than anyone so this rapid shift felt off to her. To have him put so little thought into something so big. Which was made all the harder because she couldn't help but hope that moving could be the answer.

"You could stay put," he said, snagging a crocheted afghan off the chair beside them and draping it over her shoulders. "Or you could move to my ranch and we wouldn't have to say goodbye at all," he repeated his offer, holding her gaze with his.

For a moment, she had a vision of George playing with horses. Waking up next to the man she'd trusted most for all of her adult life. Was he serious? Could he really be ready for something like that after breaking things off with Emily so recently? The possibility was scary, but she couldn't deny that it called to her too.

But was she even interpreting his words correctly? She couldn't afford to make a mistake.

"To be clear, are you asking me to move in with you? As a couple?" Such a big move made her stomach churn with butterflies. And yes, a stirring of hope.

"Yeah, I guess I am."

He *guessed*? Her vision evaporated like a soap bubble in the wind. Her tender hopes withering. What a rousing endorsement for cohabitation.

"You're still reeling from your breakup." Congratulating herself on the evenness of her tone, she hugged the afghan closer around her, drawing her knees to her chest. She refused to let this conversation derail into something that could hurt her. Or him. She cared about Riley even if they weren't on the same page. "This isn't the time to make such a big decision."

He frowned, a tight expression working on his lips and furrowing his brow. Fire crackled in the space of his breath before he replied, "Do you think I'm only suggesting this because we had sex?"

Amazing sex. "Aren't you?"

Even as the words left her lips, she could feel her control on her emotions waver, making her tone sharper than she intended. Because sex did change things. But that could be a good thing, right?

Riley dragged in a long breath, his gaze steady. "I would be lying if I said I don't want a repeat to what happened today. But sex—great sex—aside, you are my friend. And I'm going to miss you and George when I move. Whether you're in my bed or living in the guesthouse, I would look forward to seeing you when I wake up each day."

The defensiveness melted from her shoulders like snow in spring. She appreciated his words. She echoed those feelings. "That's sweet."

"I understand things are moving fast—even though we've known each other for nearly fifteen years. This is a new level for us." He smoothed her hair from her face, his touch gentle, the calluses a sweet abrasion against her cheek. "And make no mistake, I would like nothing more than to have sex with you again. And again."

Her body stirred, heart rate kicking up at his touch. She wanted him too, but she also needed to hear whatever he had to say. His offer was too big of a deal to get lost in a haze of passion. The price of choosing wrong could be costly, painful.

Licking her lips, she ventured, "I want that too. But we should talk about this, shouldn't we? Before we fall under the spell of something that could make us lose perspective even more?"

He stroked her hair. Soothing. Stirring. "Lucy, if you need us to take more time, I will gladly go at whatever pace will make you most comfortable."

She couldn't deny that the rapid shift from Emily to her made Lucy...uncomfortable. But she also couldn't ignore the chemistry that had just rocked her world. If she pushed him away now, how awkward would it be if she changed her mind later?

And then the logical solution came to her. She didn't have to choose now. "What if we don't decide that today? We have a week left on the vacation. What if we make the most of the rest of our week together and…date?"

"Date?" He repeated the word like it was a foreign concept.

"Yes, let's be a couple, get to know each other in that way. It's a new dynamic, one that should be fun. Let's not cheat ourselves out of the romance." She tugged at his shirt, the familiar and new pull between them, the new turn to their relationship, filling her with excitement. "And just so you know, odds are good at the end of the first date, you'll get lucky. What do you say?"

She waited, her heart speeding, his answer suddenly more important than she would have imagined a week ago.

"On one condition."

Her heartbeat tripped over itself. "What would that be?"

His dark eyes lit with excitement and a hint of suggestiveness. "I get to plan the dates."

"Deal," she said, taking delight in the glimmer in his eyes.

He swept her into his arms. "You won't be sorry. I love a challenge."

"Well," she answered, playing her fingers along his chest, "you can tell me all about your plans while we're showering. Together."

Swiping steam off the bathroom mirror, Riley sidestepped Lucy as they jockeyed for space to get prepped for their evening out.

He had enjoyed every minute of the past five days with Lucy. But New Year's Eve was approaching fast and they were no closer to a serious conversation. Every time he broached the subject of his move, she shut him down.

To be fair, he found himself easily distracted when she started taking his clothes off—or hers.

Although, at the moment, they were putting clothes on.

Lucy gathered her hair into a half updo, letting her red waves fall freely to frame her face. Effortless, beautiful, and perfect for the date night with the O'Briens and Archers this evening at a restaurant in Gatlinburg. Prior to this, they'd gone on dates alone or participated in a workshop at the ranch.

They'd even fallen into a routine of morning horseback riding right after she checked in with George. Lucy wasn't ready to climb a narrow mountain trail, but she'd graduated to paths through the forest. She even admitted to enjoying their rides.

Even though they'd originally planned for him to make the dates, they'd ended up alternating. She'd signed them up for chocolate making and karaoke. He'd selected some activities to deepen bonds— one of them required them to create a vision board for the coming year. He also steered his choices toward events that would show her how much she could enjoy life on a horse farm. That it wasn't all about large scary beasts.

Riley tugged on his long-sleeved black tee then fished his favorite flannel from the steel plated drawer in the bathroom, and switched places with her in a wordless negotiation of small space. "What's been your favorite activity this week?"

She lifted a finger in the area, miming a light-bulb moment. "Opening my binders."

"Funny." Fastening his flannel's buttons one by one, he admired the way her skinny jeans hugged her curves, that way her legs looked in those thigh-high black boots.

Lucy arched a brow, opening a drawer to pull out her small bag of makeup. "You shouldn't be so obvious with your hints."

"What do you think I'm hinting?"

She turned to face him, leaning back against the sink. "Trying to steer me to discuss what happens after we leave here."

"Why would you think that?"

"Aside from the frequent horseback rides—which you know I have actually enjoyed—every activity you've chosen had to do with long-range planning and partnerships." She uncapped her eyeliner as she leveled a look at him.

"I'm not that transparent."

She rolled her eyes as she turned back to the mirror. "Aren't you?"

"I don't mean to be."

She popped her mouth open while she drew a wing on her right eye. Then her left before holding his gaze in the mirror. Those green eyes even more intense. "This is never going to work if we can't be at ease around each other."

Never? That was harsh. "You're the one who said we need to date each other."

"Date. Not act like total strangers who just met online. There has to be something between first meeting and moving in together." She swept pink lip gloss over her mouth, then pursed her lips together with a smack.

Hmm. He forced his brain back to the conversation, not easy to do when he wanted to kiss and take her back to bed. "What do you propose we do differently on this dating plan?"

"Just talk to me the way you would have before."

He stepped up behind her, hands on her hips, pressing the words to her skin, a growl against her ear. "Except I never would have complimented your butt before this week. Now if you want me to cut that out…"

Laughing, she leaned back against his chest. "Compliments are acceptable."

The tableau of the two of them in the mirror looked so right he wondered how he'd missed it before. But now that he'd wised up, he planned to do everything in his power to persuade her to join him when he moved.

Gazing out the window of the aerial tramway, Lucy took in the slopes and far-off buildings of Gatlinburg. The dusting of snow late in the day had settled in the twilight, turning the ground beneath her into a winter wonderland.

From this height, problems seemed far away and manageable. Kind of like when she used her binders to generate order from the dollops of chaos life had seemed intent on handing her again and again.

She angled forward to see Nina. The blonde's

hair fell in loose waves around her face—humidity sure didn't wreak havoc on her hair. Hollie stood on the other side of her while Douglas, Jacob and Riley gathered at the center of the many windowed tramway car, talking and pointing to sites on the ground so very far below.

The evening out with the O'Briens and the Archers had felt very…normal. But in a way she'd never experienced. She and Colin hadn't shared any friends in common. She'd told herself it was a good thing that they each had their own interests and social circles, while somehow missing the point that they had no overlap.

Or maybe she hadn't wanted to see because that would have led her to question all the time he spent away.

Nerves pattered in her stomach. She knew Riley was ten times the man that Colin had hoped to be. But that didn't take away the fear of entering… what?

A relationship. There was no use in denying it to herself. They were headed into territory that rattled her.

But she could at least delay dealing with it for a couple more days. "I would imagine you've accumulated quite a few interesting stories about guests over the years."

Hollie tilted her head to the left, dark hair spilling over the front of her camel-tone peacoat. "Good stories, and challenging ones. Helping people heal their rifts doesn't always go smoothly. Once, these twin guys came for a family reunion. The two hadn't been close in years. And every activity, they found ways to humiliate the other. Another time, a couple came to us a year after their child had been killed by a drunk driver. Their pain was still so tangible. The husband refused to participate in any relationship-building exercise so the wife ended up spending her time crying at the spa. Still, we have more success stories—more experiences building and rebuilding connection than not. Nina can speak to that firsthand."

Lucy leaned forward on her elbows, wondering what magic Hollie O'Brien and Nina Archer had tapped into to make their marriages work in spite of hardships.

Nina played with the ring on her finger, toggling the princess-cut diamond back and forth absently as she spoke. "I'm glad we had this chance to just relax before we hit the road."

"You've had a working holiday," Lucy said, "taking all those amazing photos."

Nina shrugged, adjusted her pink scarf. "This is the life we've signed up for being a part of the Top

Dog enterprise. And of course, the horse-breeding ranch won't have days off, so it's nice you and Riley had this chance to relax."

"We're not a couple," she corrected automatically.

"You may not have been a couple when you got here, but you sure seem to be one now." Nina smiled knowingly.

Were they? Could they keep the magic they'd found here? The thought of wrecking their friendship scared her to her toes.

"No comment." Lucy willed herself not to blush.

Nina smiled just before her husband called out to her from the other side of the enclosed car. Touching Lucy and Hollie on their shoulders to excuse herself, Nina took careful steps across the swaying car toward her husband. Tucking against him with easy familiarity, she followed the point of his fingers outside to something beyond the scope of Lucy's vision.

Seeing Nina so happy filled Lucy with sparks of pure admiration and even a little envy. To grow with someone? The rarest kind of bond.

Pressing a hand to an ache in her chest, Lucy looked away. Soft murmurs from Nina, Douglas, Jacob and Riley mingled with the young family of three at the other end of the sky tram. A girl of about eight pressed her mittened palms to her cheeks, squealing as her mother pointed to a herd of deer darting beneath a string of outdoor Christmas lights.

Lucy shifted, leaning back against the seat, turning toward Hollie. "Thank you for inviting us to come along."

"It's nice to have an evening out as a regular couple. Thank you for reaching out." Hollie glanced down at her hands for a moment, her hair shielding her eyes from view. "This holiday has been particularly difficult for us. After the last fertility treatment ended in a miscarriage, we decided to adopt. We became parents to a little boy, then the birth mother changed her mind."

Her soft voice didn't hide the deep pain of the words.

"Oh no, I'm so sorry," Lucy gasped softly. "I can't even imagine what you've been through."

Hollie tipped her face toward the darkening landscape. Silver shone in her eyes for a moment. Lucy touched her arm lightly, her heart aching for the woman's grief. While she'd never experienced that pain, the depth of loss for an imagined, desired future was pain she knew too well.

"This would have been our son's first Christmas." Hollie held up a hand. "It *is* his first Christmas. He's not dead. We're just never going to see him again."

Lucy bit her lip, unsure what to say when there was no way to comfort that kind of loss.

Hollie shook her head. "Please, there's no need to say anything. There is nothing anyone can say to make this better. Even Jacob and I struggle with how to comfort each other. I know it may seem strange that I'm sharing this with you when we barely know each other. But you truly are a kindred spirit and it feels good to talk about it, rather than bottling things up all the time."

Lucy understood what she meant. She felt the same.

"We've both been let down by life in a big way and somehow managed to forge ahead." She looked over at Riley. Even in the dim lighting, there was no missing his hard muscled body...or his kind eyes. "Although I can't claim to have done it on my own."

Riley came through for her again and again.

"During the early miscarriages Jacob and I could turn to each other, then we doubled down with determination to carry a child to term. When the adoption failed, we didn't have anything left to give each other. Ironic, isn't it, that we've made it our mission to help others repair broken relationships."

Lucy wondered if they'd used helping others as a distraction from dealing with their own problems. Was that what Riley had been doing by inviting her on this trip—"helping" her with her Christmas crisis to avoid thinking of his own? If so, she'd been a horrible friend not to have noticed sooner.

Maybe that was the missing piece. She needed to be there for him in a more proactive way, encouraging him to open up.

Except that also came with the fear she might discover that his willingness to enter into a relationship with her was reactionary. Driven by circumstances and not because of a deeper love. But it was a risk she had to take as his friend. And she needed to do it sooner rather than later. Because there was no escaping the ticking clock.

Their time away from the world here at the Top Dog Dude Ranch was drawing to a close.

Riley tucked Lucy to his side, taking in the panoramic view, the perfect romantic mood to usher in the rest of their evening.

He'd never been one for heights, but this aerial tramway trek was changing his mind. Of course, it probably had something to do with his arm around Lucy. Now the O'Briens and the Archers had meandered to the other side of the car.

Which left Lucy and him alone to take in the twinkling white lights and mountain silhouettes.

And so far, so good. Sure, he'd known Lucy for about fifteen years. And while they'd always been able to work a room together, his heart and hope soared at how natural dinner had felt. Twining hands. Laughing with other couples.

Simple.

For a change.

His thumb stroked the outside of Lucy's arm. So easy to fall into the rhythm as he looked out the large-framed windows to the snow-covered mountainside.

Lucy rested her head against his shoulder, her cinnamon scent tempting his every breath as she nestled into his chest, playing with the button on his checkered flannel shirt. "I'm sorry if I haven't listened to your hurt enough on this trip. I feel like I've made it all about me, which pushed you right back into old habits of taking care of me."

Well, that wasn't exactly the vibe he was angling for. He searched for a benign answer that would allow him to steer back toward dating and moving in together. "I like to think we take care of each other."

He pulled her closer.

"I'm not so sure about that." She took his hands,

green eyes searching. "You were there for me when Colin and I split. I fell short in supporting you. You even had to convince me I would be doing you a favor by coming on this extravagant trip."

What was she getting at? He knew he was missing something, some angle that escaped him, but for the life of him he couldn't think what she might be driving at. But he recognized this evening was veering off the romance path. He knew how to quickly correct course in the arena.

But those skills failed him now in this setting. "Uhm, my pride was hurt most of all. Now can we change the subject?"

Her jaw set with determination. He recognized the look on her face all too well.

"Uh-uh, Riley. You're not going to brush me aside that easily this time." She took his face in her hands. "I need for you to hear how sorry I am."

"And I need for you to hear that I chose poorly with Emily." He clasped her wrists, keeping his voice low. "That's on me. Not you."

Her eyebrows pinched together, concern flooding her green eyes. A hint of past pain tugged at her lip in a way that made Riley want to protect her from the world. And just like that, he watched her push her own troubles down, down, down. Just like she always did.

"You've taken on the pain of my bad choices. How is this different that I want to help you with yours?"

"Because I wasn't married to her so it's not as big of a deal," he said simply.

What he'd been through didn't come close to the betrayal Lucy had suffered. He pressed his mouth to hers to stop her from denying it. She was always downplaying her struggles. He knew firsthand how brave she was. She didn't need to prove anything to him.

He palmed her back, savoring the feel of her, of a simple kiss that couldn't go further here with others around. But he certainly didn't take for granted the opportunity to kiss her, to be a part of a couple with this incredible woman.

From a couple of feet away, a throat clearing echoed. Once. Twice. Riley twisted to see Jacob gripping his cell phone. "Uhm, hey you two, I hate to be the bearer of bad news, but I just got a message from the ranch…"

Lucy gasped. "George?" Already she was reaching for her cell phone. "Are they looking for me?"

Jacob shook his head. "Not you, Lucy. The message is for Riley." He scrubbed a hand along the back of his neck sheepishly. "Emily has arrived and she is looking for you."

Chapter Thirteen

Lucy climbed out of the O'Briens' van, stepping into the snowy yard in front of the cabin. Numb. She'd been frozen on the inside since the moment she'd heard about Emily's arrival. The ride back to the ranch with the O'Briens and the Archers had been a blur, their nervous small talk swirling all around her.

And Riley?

He'd been silent as well, other than telling Lucy he had no intention of calling Emily before they returned. Anything his former fiancée had to say would need to be shared in person.

So here they stood. Outside their cabin, while

Emily sat on the porch in a rocker as if she belonged. Her pale blond hair elegantly styled in romantic curls that pooled down her designer black trench coat.

Anger rose in Lucy. Emily had abdicated any right to this place when she'd stomped all over Riley's heart by cheating with another man.

And underneath that anger sat a layer of fear. What if he returned to Emily? Not only would Lucy lose her friendship with Riley, but also this new aspect to their relationship that she'd only just realized was so deeply important to her. She shot a quick glance at Riley, trying to see what he was thinking. But his face was inscrutable, giving no hint to his feelings.

Riley stepped out of the O'Briens' van that sported a Top Dog logo on the side. "Thanks for the evening out," he said to Jacob. "Sorry to shut it down early."

"No worries," Jacob answered, casting a glance between them and the porch where Emily was seated. "We understand. Let us know if there's anything we can do. Good night to you both." He tipped his Stetson before rolling up the window.

The van drove off into the night, puffs from the tailpipe dissipating into the cold air until they faded from sight along the path into the forest.

Leaving Lucy and Riley alone with Emily.

Lucy tamped down the urge to throw herself between them. To tell Emily exactly what she thought of her showing up here. Now. But she knew those weren't just protective, friendly instincts. It was an impulse born of her new and complicated feelings for Riley that they hadn't worked through yet. Still, she had no right to come between him and his ex-girlfriend if the woman wanted him back.

Did she?

Emily pushed on the arms of the rocker, standing. She picked her way down the steps toward Riley across the lawn from the cabin. She kept her eyes well off Lucy. Emily eyed him warily.

Gritting her teeth, Lucy breathed through her worst instincts and rested a hand on Riley's arm. She needed to be a good friend. "I should just go inside. Or you two can go inside to talk and I'll stay out of your way by walking Pickles."

It was probably better that she find a productive outlet for her nervous energy.

"No," he said brusquely. "We are not going in. Walk Pickles if you would like, but I want you close."

Ugh. She would rather crawl into a snowbank naked than listen to this conversation. Awkward didn't even begin to cover it. "Fine then. I'll walk Pickles."

She strode to the porch, angling past Emily. By the time Lucy grabbed Pickles's leash and stepped back outside, a bit of Riley and Emily's conversation floated along the night breeze. Even though Lucy had offered to stay away, she couldn't help but listen, her heart in her throat.

Riley stuffed his hands in his coat pockets. "Emily, what are you doing here?"

Pickles tugged on the leash, pulling her along the cabin's side. The pup seemed intent on helping Lucy hear the conversation as he sniffed the ground. He was always a sweet pup, but since they'd gotten to the dude ranch, Pickles's empathy skills were on overdrive. Was there something in the water here?

"I'm so sorry, Riley. Please forgive me." Emily clutched his arm, her voice wobbling.

In years past, Emily's face had always maintained a kind of porcelain elegance and grace. Tonight, in the subdued starlight and Christmas lights, Lucy recognized a different emotion. Something like devastation. A brokenness and loneliness in the curve of her lips that reminded Lucy of so many nights spent waiting for Colin to come home. A face that reflected genuine hurt.

The woman took a steadying breath, but Lucy saw the ways Emily's mouth twitched groundward. A fresh urge to walk away from this conversation rose up in Lucy, but Riley had asked that of her and she intended to honor his request. No matter how uncomfortable.

"I shouldn't have been so suspicious of you and Lucy." Emily sniffled, swiping at her face impatiently. "It was wrong of me. She's your friend and I should have trusted you. I'm not making any excuses other than that I got scared and I made a mistake."

For Lucy, the admission sent her own senses spinning. The conversation between Riley and Emily suddenly sounded distant as she tried to comprehend what Riley's ex had just said. That Emily had been jealous of her and Riley, enough to push her into a breakup. Up until a couple of weeks ago, that statement would have elicited a deep belly laugh from her.

But things had changed.

He carefully shrugged off her touch and crossed his arms. "That might be a believable story if it weren't for the other guy."

Emily inhaled sharply while she nodded. Tears glimmered in her eyes. She took another deep breath and pressed her hand to her heart. "I was just trying to make you jealous because I was envious of Lucy." She shot a glance her way sheepishly, the anguish twisting her lips genuine. "It was childish of me and you deserve better. I know that you and Lucy have never done anything to deserve what I said."

Guilt tweaked as she thought of all they'd done in the past days, sex and dates that would give Emily every cause to be jealous. A twinge of empathy tugged at Lucy harder than Pickles pulled on the leash. It was easier to be angry with the woman from a distance.

Emily turned back to Riley, her hands together in a plea. "Please, I just want a chance to make it up to you. Whatever I can do to get you back. Say the word."

Riley shook his head. "I'm here with Lucy."

"You brought her because I let you down." Emily swiped away a tear.

Lucy noticed the resolve and ways Emily was trying to be accountable for the mistake that had cut Riley deep. Something Colin had never done. Even beyond that, the woman was here. Making a real effort.

Nodding, Emily continued, "I understand that and I deserve it. It's okay that the two of you are friends. I see how wrong I was. We can still get married and I won't let your friendship with her come between us ever again."

Emily had been suffering with a species of jealousy and unease that Lucy had the great misfortune of knowing intimately. She knew that pain and hated it for her. Even though she still felt anger rise in her chest for the hurt Emily had caused Riley. Her best friend. Her rock. The best man she'd ever known.

"No, we can't get married, ever," Riley said emphatically. "Because you were right. I'm in love with Lucy."

The surprise on Emily's face over his declaration echoed the shock Riley felt all the way to his toes. What stunned him even more than the fact he'd said those words out loud?

The words were true.

He was in love with Lucy. Of course he was. It had always been about Lucy for him. He'd just been too focused on being her friend that he hadn't taken the time to see the layers of feelings—of love—underneath.

Had she heard what he said? She was across the snow-covered lawn, climbing back up the cabin steps with Pickles. He would have to talk to her regardless of whether she'd heard or not, but first, he needed to send Emily on her way.

And he needed to be kinder about ending things than blurting out that he loved someone else. Emily had been right to be jealous. He'd done her a disservice by proposing in the first place.

Stepping toward Emily, Riley extended a hand, touching her arm. For the first time in weeks, since before she'd kissed that other cowboy, he really looked at her, and saw the pain and worry etched in her features. "I'm sorry, more than I can say, for hurting you. But you have to know there can never be a future for the two of us as a couple."

Emily blinked fast, her eyes glinting with unshed tears. "I knew it," she said, swiping her fingers across her cheeks. Emily's voice dropped an octave. Nothing accusatory. Just a kind of bone-deep understanding. Her voice cracked as her eyes looked to her boots. "I was just so sad over Christmas that I tried to convince myself I was wrong about the two of you."

Riley's boot crunched in the snow as he retreated back a step from Emily. His brow furrowed as the understanding of the last two years of his life seemed to shift. "I never meant to hurt you. Our time together meant a lot to me, as well."

"We gave it a good try, though." Her smile bittersweet, she tugged the tie on her coat.

He nodded. "I hope you'll find someone who's worthy of you."

She snorted on a laugh, eyes flaring wide with pain and understanding. "It's going to be a long time before I'm ready to jump back in the saddle. I think I'm due a mind-blowing meaningless fling."

Her spunk right now made him smile. They'd been together for over two years, known each other even longer. He was going to miss her. She gave him a quick hug, then walked back to her car as fast as a person could on an icy drive. The engine started and she tore up the road, out of his life.

Endings were rough, even when they were for the best. His mind went back to the day Lucy had come to him, her heart broken over the end of her marriage…

Wondering what had been so important that Lucy sent him an SOS text not to leave until she could get there, that she needed him, Riley lifted up Sugar's leg to remove the dirt and small stones from around the frog of the Appaloosa gelding's inner hoof. Sugar was his favorite barrel-racer horse but had the most sensitive hooves he'd ever seen.

Footfalls came from behind him, echoing off the

concrete in the six-stall horse barn. Upside down and between his legs, he saw Lucy approach.

He set the hoof down, pivoting to face his best friend, concerned, ready to hear what was on her mind. Moving past the well-worn rope cross ties, he took in the sight of Lucy. She stopped in front of him. Eyes rimmed with red. A sure sign that something was very wrong.

Concern surged in his chest as he went to ask what was wrong. Before he could speak, she chewed her lip once, twice. Exhaled and blurted her news out. "I've left Colin."

About time. "What happened?"

"I found out he's been cheating on me." Her story tumbled from her mouth. "All that traveling was just a cover. Half the time he was staying at hotels the next county over. I found his secret credit card and then one of his 'girlfriends' confirmed everything. He still tried to bluff and say it was for business." Hugging her stomach, she nearly doubled up from the weight of her words.

Anger surged through him as he pulled her close, her cinnamon perfume mixing with the smell of salty tears.

"Lucy, I'm so sorry. You were too good for him."

"It's been going on for a long time." Her eyes flooded with fresh tears. "He was with another

woman the day George was born. That's why I couldn't reach him."

Shock gutted him. That was lower than he would have expected from even Colin.

Water leaked from her eyes, a river of pain streaming down her cheeks. The water pooled on his shirt as he stroked her back.

If Colin had been standing in front of him right now, he would have pummeled him into the ground for hurting her this way. She deserved so much better. She needed him and he would be here for her, help while she cried out her grief.

His news would have to wait. This wasn't the time to tell Lucy that he'd proposed to Emily—and she'd accepted.

Riley's declaration to Emily had sent a ripple of shock waves through Lucy so strong she almost dropped Pickles's leash. He couldn't be serious.

As she stood watching him through the window ten minutes later, she still grappled to process the words. He loved her? He'd never told her so. Never hinted that…

And just as fast as the words registered, she realized he had to be making an excuse to send Emily on her way for good. And it had worked, since she'd left before Lucy could even unclip Pickles's leash. Riley, on the other hand, still stood outside, snow drifting from the sky and piling on his broad shoulders that she'd leaned on far too often. What was he thinking? How did he feel?

And how did *she* feel?

Like she was about to have a panic attack.

She leaned against the back of the couch, toying with the soft fabric in an attempt to ground her swimming thoughts. Had Riley really been using a pretend vow of love for Lucy to push away Emily? The idea cut something in Lucy's heart. Her throat worked on a swallow, anxiety bubbling up too fast.

Twitchy, hurt and confusion leaving her agitated, she paced by the big picture window, pausing only to click on the fireplace. Small flames sputtered to life drenching the cabin in warm tones that did little to thaw the icy shards of pain inside her.

Finally, Riley turned toward the cabin, moonlight streaming over his angular face, the lines set harder than normal. He took slow, deliberate steps back to the cabin, his boots punching holes in the snow. He climbed to the porch, to the door, crossing the threshold.

Placing his Stetson on the table by the door, he watched her without speaking. His eyes never left her as he shrugged out of his jacket. Tension crackled through the room. She hated the loss of the ease they'd shared earlier when they'd gotten dressed in the bathroom with such hopes for their date night.

Lucy's nerves frayed. She couldn't wait for him to speak. Not with this hurt and anger sparking in every direction inside her. She crossed her arms over her chest while Pickles circled around her feet. "I know you told Emily that you love me in order to save face."

Her heart pounded.

He walked to her, each footfall a gentle thud against the planks. "So you heard that."

Oh. Wow. He hadn't known for sure? She could have pretended nothing happened and just moved forward with the rest of the trip.

Just as quickly as the thought formed, she dismissed it. There was no going back for them. They'd played a risky game with their friendship these past days. "I'm not holding you to anything. We've helped each other out more than once. It's what friends do."

He lifted an eyebrow, hand bracing on the back of the sofa. "Friends? Lucy, we've moved well past that now, don't you think?"

She agreed, but not in the way she knew he'd meant. She backed away, noting yet again how fast this had all moved between them. Too fast. "Friends with benefits, remember?"

A deep swallow did little to push down the pain hammering away at her heart. There seemed to be no way to sidestep the impending damage. No way to organize their emotions. No binder for this territory.

"I'm telling you—it's more than that." He lifted her hand, stopping her retreat. "I meant what I said out there."

Meant what he'd said?

He couldn't even say the words now and she was supposed to believe he loved her that way, romantically, in the way she deserved? She should be glad though, because if he'd given his heart to her—so soon after Emily—she would have to sift through her own mixed-up feelings.

"You're just confused after the ugly breakup with Emily, and what we have is…comfortable." Although at the moment, her feelings were far from comfortable.

Her ragged heartbeat knocked against her ribs. Pickles parked himself into a sit in front of her, tail wagging as he cocked his head to the side. Sensing the distress again?

Riley cradled her face in his hands. "Why can't you just accept that we may have something special?"

His touch tempted her, making her yearn to

throw caution to the wind and take the words at face value, even when her every instinct screamed that this didn't make sense.

Not now. "Riley, it's not that simple."

Grasping his hands, she pulled them from her face and stared deep into his brown eyes.

"I believe that it is." His square jaw flexed. "Every person you meet isn't Colin. Or your father."

His words hit her like a slap. All her softer feelings, the inclination to lean into his touch evaporated.

She stepped away, hands on her hips, staring him down. "That's rich, coming from you. You've used your past with your dad's addictions as an excuse not to commit."

"I was ready to commit to Emily," he countered.

"Puh-lease. Like she was ever a serious threat to your heart." Pickles leaned against her legs with a small inquisitive whine.

Riley's eyebrows shot upward. "And yet you said nothing to warn me."

"It wasn't my place." Was there something to what he'd said about her avoiding the possibility of a relationship with him out of fear that she would be hurt? Or had she worried telling him of her concerns would make him leave? "Not any more than I would have listened to you. But you already know that. Which means there's only one reason for this conversation. You're picking a fight with me."

No doubt he needed space after how fast things had moved this week. She could understand that well enough since she'd been feeling overwhelmed too. Only now that he was pushing her away, pointing out her flaws, she wasn't so sure she could stand the thought of things fraying between them.

"Picking a fight? I'm the one who asked you to move in with me," he pointed out, his voice rising in exasperation.

How dare he be upset with her? He seemed to have conveniently forgotten that he'd asked her to move in during what should have been his honeymoon with another woman who he'd only left because she cheated. That reminder stiffened her spine and resolve. They'd moved too fast, and she needed to call it to a halt now before they crashed and burned their entire relationship.

"Well, consider yourself officially off the hook, Riley Stewart. Once the snow stops, I'm leaving."

For good.

Chapter Fourteen

Riley couldn't recall ever feeling this pessimistic at a New Year's Eve party. Had it only been a week since he and Lucy were in this same barn, wearing ugly sweaters thinking that their biggest problem was figuring how to handle the attraction between them?

Now he wasn't even sure if she would be in his life after the countdown to midnight. The rope banner spelling out Happy New Year! over the country band seemed more of a joke than a promise of good fortune on a bell stroke.

He'd slept on the sofa last night while she stayed in the bedroom, snow forcing them both to remain inside. He knew her well enough to realize there was no convincing her to change her mind then. She would need time to organize her thoughts, much like she did with data in her binders. Keeping his mouth closed and giving her space, he just hoped that snow kept the road closed a while longer so he could find a way to plead his case.

For now, he stood on the edge of the party, listening to the upbeat country-rock song by the live band—"Barks and Backroads." People swirled around him. And not for the first time this trip, he envied the glimpses of ease he saw in the other couples dressed in fringe and cowboy boots.

Riley wanted that life with Lucy. The love and warm devotion. The certainty of knowing a partner had your back. He knew that they'd been on the knife's edge of coming together as seamlessly as the mac-and-cheese Nina scooped onto her plate across the barn for her kids.

The Archer twins dressed in matching red bandannas, chambray shirts and red cowgirl boots skipped across the dance floor. They stopped for a moment to jump up and down, singing along to the chorus before making their way to the side room where a "kids only" New Year's countdown party was taking place.

How he wished George was here to enjoy himself. Though if he were in the mode of wishing, Riley would spare a wish on making things right with Lucy.

A tap on the microphone drew his attention to the stage.

"Here at the Top Dog Dude Ranch, we're all about connections." The twentysomething singer with dusky brown hair said, leaning in to the mic, "If you are too, make some noise!"

People milling about the barbecue spread paused, turning to answer with whoops and whistles, the crowd all in tune with each other and the mood of the moment. Connection was vital. Riley knew this from his days in the saddle.

Connection to Lucy? It was everything.

He couldn't imagine his life without her. And he could only blame himself for hiding from his love for so long until he may well have missed his chance with her.

Perhaps there was something to what she'd said about him avoiding deeper emotions because of his father. The thought of immersing himself in turmoil—and possibly letting down a family the way his dad had let them down—tore him up.

"Hey," Jacob called, tipping his Stetson and setting down his plate of finger foods on the yellow tablecloth next to the sunflowers arranged in a cowboy-boot vase. "Is everything okay?"

Talk about a déjà vu moment. Hadn't he been standing in much the same spot Christmas Eve wondering what to do next when Jacob had joined him?

Although Jacob had helped him through then. Maybe he would have answers now.

Riley pulled on the brim of his black Stetson. "I've screwed up."

"I assume this has something to do with your former fiancée making a surprise appearance," he said in an even, knowing tone.

Riley's eyes skimmed the crowd, searching for a whisper of Lucy, a reminder of her presence since she'd been here with him just last week. Instead, he only saw Hollie and Nina standing together in front of a haystack styled with a bridle, lasso and tall, sky-reaching sunflowers.

"I told Emily it's over and that my heart belongs to Lucy."

"Then what's the problem?" Jacob asked.

"Lucy doesn't believe me." Riley drummed his finger on the lip of the mason jar filled with lemonade.

"To be fair," Jacob said, leaning back, putting one booted foot against the wall, "you did make a mighty fast shift from Emily to Lucy. I could see how she would worry about being a rebound relationship."

Rebound? "Lucy and I have known each other for nearly fifteen years."

Jacob stayed quiet, returning the wave of a passing couple. The silence stretched until finally he said, "I don't know how helpful my advice would be."

"You've heard about my plans every step of the way buying the ranch. And you help people every day here." Riley also realized how adrift he was since every other time he'd needed a friendly ear, he'd gone to Lucy. "I'm out of ideas and in need of advice."

"Alright then. If you've been friends for that long, why the romantic shift now? I could see how she might question your feelings, given how quickly it came on after your breakup."

The answer was simple. "This is the first time we've both been free at the same time. I wanted her to be happy so much, I was willing to put aside my own feelings rather than share my concerns about Colin when she got married."

How many times over the years had their timing been off? Their kiss before school ended when he'd needed to break free from his dysfunctional family. Her marriage. His engagement. They'd been at cross-purposes too long. But not anymore.

"Have you mentioned that to her?" Jacob gave him a level stare.

"I only just realized it myself." He'd been too busy enjoying the incredible experience of being with Lucy that he hadn't stopped to pick through the whys of it. Now he also wondered if they'd held back deeper feelings in the past out of fear of losing each other altogether.

He could also see why she would have been hurt—even insecure—after the way Colin had treated her. He should have been more sensitive to that and reassured her.

Whatever it took to reassure her—however long—he was in. Because he saw now why no other relationship had worked for him. His heart belonged to Lucy, and it always would.

He turned to Jacob again. "While you're offering advice, do you have any thoughts about how I can win her back?"

"It just so happens," Jacob said, grinning, "I have just the idea for a romantic New Year's celebration."

"George, sweetie, it's mighty late. What are you doing still awake?" Lucy picked her way around icy patches outside the barn, holding her phone up while sticking to the spaces the floodlights illuminated.

Noise poured from the open doors, the Top Dog New Year's party in full swing. She shrugged her shoulders, attempting to sink farther into her big wool coat to brace against the chill of night.

"Daddy and Talia said I could stay up," he paused, yawning, "and I don't want to miss all the fireworks."

She held back the urge to remind Colin of how cranky George got when his schedule was disrupted. Her son was making happy memories. She would deal with the rest when he got home.

Provided the snow eased, this would be her last night at the Top Dog Dude Ranch. Her throat tightened.

"Okay, be sure to remind your dad to take lots of pictures and send them to me." She cupped the phone in her mittened hand.

"I will. I miss you, Mommy." George brought the tablet close to his eyes to emphasize each I statement.

Then his deep red curls bounced as he looked behind him to where a party unfolded. In the background, people around the living room with cathedral ceilings held plates filled with food, Colin with his arm around Talia.

Memories of Riley holding her that way made her ache with the pain of a fresh loss. A loss that would be so much deeper than her broken marriage if she couldn't salvage something—anything—with Riley.

Lucy blinked away the hurt and pulled her focus back to her son. "Miss you too. And I love you. So much." She blew kisses to him. "I can't wait to see you very soon."

Music from the barn grew louder as they started an upbeat tune. An older couple in complementary Stetsons and fringe vests laughed together as they walked past on their way out.

George's blue eyes went wide as he put one hand to his cheek. "Yep. Tell Riley I said hi. And give him a big hug from me."

Her mouth dried right up. Panic threatened to creep into her even-keeled nature. Conjuring her last bit of mom superpower, she gave him a bright smile. "Uh-huh."

"Good night. Happy New Year. Love you—"

The phone line disconnected before he could finish the sentence.

And she wanted to cry, even though her tears would likely freeze on her cheeks. How was she going to tell George that she'd pushed away Riley, their rock since the day George had been born? She'd thought the breakup of her marriage had been the worst thing to happen to her.

She'd been wrong.

Lucy pulled the coat tighter around her before adjusting the cream-colored cowgirl hat Riley had bought her a few days ago. The heartbreak over losing Riley surpassed anything she'd ever felt. Standing alone outside the barn full of happy people only deepened the loneliness she'd imposed on herself. Why had she shoved away the possibility of happiness with both hands? Was she that scared? That unable to take another chance in life?

Tipping her head back to look up at the stars, she wished she had the answers. Could there have been something to what Riley had said about her rejecting him in order to keep her heart safe? That she was wary of real commitment because of her father and then Colin?

She thought of her binders and how she'd tried to organize her life. That if she planned for every possibility, she could protect herself from failure.

Yet, life—and feelings—weren't that neat. In fact, they were often so very unpredictable and messy, part of what made them so exciting.

And Riley had been bringing excitement and

smiles to her life since the day he'd strode into her ninth grade class. He'd been there for her, catching her every time she stumbled, showing her the lasting power of true love.

If ever she could have used some Top Dog magic, this was that moment. Tears burned the backs of her eyes and she bit her lip to keep them from falling. She needed help.

She needed Riley.

Then over the party sounds of laughter and music, she heard bells. A soft jingling that slowly grew. Followed by the swish of snow and ice. The rhythmic beat of horse hooves. The sounds swelled louder and louder, until she turned to see...

A sleigh approaching, the one that Santa had used after rappelling down the mountain. It was decked in holiday garland and bells, drawn by two draft horses.

Except Santa was nowhere to be seen. The reins were held by a tall, handsome cowboy. None other than the man who'd always made Lucy's every wish come true.

Riley.

He stopped the sleigh in a dust-up of fresh snow, then jumped down to the ground, extending his hand. "Do you need a ride?"

The scent of cedar and pine swirled. The scent of leather and man making her breath catch.

After fidgeting with the fit of her gloves and then smoothing her coat, she settled her racing heart and clasped his fingers with hers. Hope swelled inside her along with gratitude to this man for arriving when she needed him most. Just like always.

How could she have ever doubted him? "Yes, as a matter of fact, I do."

The horses snuffled white breath into the crisp night air, heavy hooves stomping in a way that made the reins jingle. She let Riley help her into the seat before adjusting the blanket over her lap. Then he rounded to the other side of the big sleigh and took his place beside her.

Lifting the reins, he looked over at her, his handsome face so strong and familiar in the moonlight. "Do you mind if I take the scenic route back to our cabin?"

Heart in her throat, she could hardly speak for the emotions inside her. But she nodded.

"I trust you," she answered. And meant it.

He exhaled hard into the cold night, the lengthy sigh telling her just how much their fight had weighed on him too. Her heart raced with anticipation—and yes, still a little apprehension. She needed to get this right. Since he seemed content to stay quiet for the moment and he appeared to have a destination in mind, she sank back in the seat.

Riley guided the horses on a trail that led them farther from the sparse lights of cabins and Christmas trees toward a dip in a valley. The lack of light made the swirls and constellations of the night sky seem brighter. Brimming with possibility as a shooting star somersaulted across the horizon.

Lucy squeezed her eyes closed, wishing with her whole heart for a future with Riley. Their easy laughter, silliness, unwavering support. She blinked her eyes open as Riley slowed the horses' merry trot.

With a flick of the reins, he brought the bay draft horses to a halt in a valley they hadn't explored yet. Before her, a mountain bravely jutted into a smattering of stars. Serenity in the stillness, the sureness of something so magnificent.

He turned in the seat to face her, lifting her hands to draw off her mittens. Then, he kissed them, one then the other. "Can you forgive me for the things I said to you?"

She clasped his hands tightly in hers, his fingers warmer than any wool. "Of course, I can, just as I know you forgive me."

"I'm glad you know that." He grinned at her, moonlight streaming down on him like a spotlight. "You've been my best friend and I always thought of you as my confidant. Except I'm learning I didn't confide in you about the things that really mattered."

"About our feelings for each other, you mean?" She acknowledged the truth that had been waiting there for them to claim for nearly fifteen years. It was time. They were ready.

And she loved this man with every bit of her being.

His heart was in his eyes. Perhaps it always had been if only she looked beyond her own fears.

"Exactly. My dad made it tough to envision family life as anything at all pleasant." His throat moved in a slow bob.

She understood better now about how the pain from his difficult past had sent him from their hometown as soon as he was old enough to escape.

Still, she had to know. "Why, then, did you propose to Emily?"

Snow flurries fell softly, the night quiet all around them.

"That's a fair question. Because I thought I was losing you and felt so alone. It was unfair to her. I see that now." He slid a hand to cup the back of her neck. "And unfair to you."

"We have struggled to get our timing right over

the years," she admitted, so very glad they'd somehow managed to synch up now. "Seems like we both chose people who wouldn't take our whole heart."

His thumb traced the backs of her knuckles. Slowly. Deliberately. He met her gaze in the moonlight.

"Well, you can rest assured, Lucy, you have my whole heart. Forever. I'm utterly and completely in love with you and look forward to cherishing you every day for the rest of my life."

The words coming from him—a man of so much honor—filled her with a certainty she'd never felt before. A solid foundation she would never, ever question.

"Oh, Riley, I'm so very glad because I love you too." Her forehead tipped to rest on his, their warm breaths mingling in the cold air as she allowed the joy of the moment to roll over. The relief. The promise of a future she'd hardly dared to dream about.

Then she lifted her face to meet those dark eyes of his again. "I love you, now," she repeated the vow again. "And always. I want to build a life with you, sharing all our tomorrows."

He drew her into his arms, his hands palming her back, his eyes on hers, the connection between them tangible. Enduring. He kissed her once, twice, lingering. Setting her senses on fire. She gripped his jacket, pulling him closer as she savored this moment before easing back with a breathy sigh.

"Is the offer still open to move in together at your ranch?" she teased, even though she already knew the answer.

Because Riley was more than the love of her life. He was still her best friend. And she understood this man better than anyone else.

"Ah, Lucy," he said as he swept aside her hat and buried his face in her hair. "Of course, I want you and George with me, in my life, in my home. Our home that we'll build together. And I hope you know that means I want us to be married, whenever the day comes that you're ready. However many dates it takes to persuade you that I'm all in on the adventure of spending our lives together. Rest assured, you're my one and only."

The snow flurries picked up speed, the sky throwing powdery confetti as if the whole mountain valley celebrated with them. She tucked against Riley, savoring the feeling of being with him.

Not just for tonight. But forever.

"Well then, my love, let the adventure begin."

She guided his head toward hers again until their mouths met just as New Year's fireworks lit the night sky. And she knew all the way to the tips of her toes…

The Top Dog magic was real.

Epilogue

One Year Later:

Riley had never imagined that once he called an end to his rodeo days, the thrills would double.

His arm around Lucy, he walked alongside her out of their barn and into the small gathering of friends from their new community who'd come to celebrate New Year's Eve with them. They'd put down roots in this little town in upstate Kentucky that they now called home, their first together.

Riley called out, "Is everyone ready for the fireworks display?"

Cheers rippled through the crowd of two dozen

adults and children. It wasn't actually midnight, but the sun had gone down and they wanted to make sure the kids could all enjoy the show.

Lucy arched up on her toes and whispered in his ear, "I'm looking forward to our personal fireworks show later."

A low laugh rumbled in his chest.

In the stillness as they gathered, awaiting the onset of bottle rockets and roman candles, Riley surveyed all they had built. All that they were still building, really.

Snow dusted the eaves of the one-story white-and-red ranch house. Large windows offered glimpses in to the fifteen-foot tree in the center of the living room. Lights twinkled almost as brightly as the stars and moon overhead.

Acres upon acres unfurled before them. Fields that belonged to him and Lucy—to the family they were creating. Snow blanketed the land now, but his heart already twitched, excited to spend every season here with his beautiful, caring, sexy best friend and wife.

Moonlight caught on the icicles on the tall pines, firs, and in the branches of the oaks. Sounds of horses knickered from the nearby thirty-stall stable and filtered through the air. This land, with its rising mountains off in the distance—sharing it all with Lucy and George was more than he ever dreamed of being a part of.

Their wedding last summer had been perfectly organized—thanks to three binders full of details. They'd married in a field of wildflowers on his ranch, her simple lace gown rippling in the wind, a bouquet of daisies in her hands.

She'd taken his breath away.

She still did.

He tucked her closer to his side. "Are you ready to ring in the New Year?"

"Last year was so amazing, I would have thought nothing could top it." Her green eyes shone up at him with the happiness he'd grown used to seeing there.

He loved her more every day, the way some old timers claimed they felt about long-term partners. He got it now. He understood the way time spent together could deepen and strengthen a bond. Making it unbreakable. All the more beautiful.

"Every day is better than the last with you because I wake up each morning even more in love with you."

Smiling, she reached up to stroke his face, her wedding band glinting in the moonlight. "Who would have thought I would marry a horse rancher?

You've helped me face my fears and find the blessings."

They'd found she had a way with horses, just as she did with dogs. Four-legged creatures were charmed by her. Pickles scampered in the snow with George. The boy's laughter carried on the night breeze as he brandished his new lightsaber he'd gotten for his fifth birthday. His party this year had been a blowout with his friends from his new kindergarten. Riley had supervised pony rides for all the little guests, complete with a cowboy hat and bandanna instead of traditional party hats.

Lucy was fostering a litter of puppies for the local shelter, and the children had squealed with delight over getting to play with the eight-week-old Labrador retriever mix pups.

Her new dog-walking venture had expanded into a dog-boarding business. She'd fenced off sections of the land, which offered the perfect places for the canine critters to enjoy their "vacation." She now employed a staff of five, and still had to turn away customers.

The Top Dog magic had spread to their lives in so many ways.

She wasn't riding as much these days. Even with her adventurous new equestrian spirit, she was taking things easier.

As per orders from her obstetrician.

Their family was growing.

His arm around her waist, Riley rested his hand along the curve of her stomach where their baby grew. George was over-the-moon excited to be a big brother. He was thriving with life on the ranch and all the wide-open spaces to play.

So was Pickles.

In moments, they would find out if they were having a boy or a girl at their New Year's Eve gender-reveal party.

He drew in a breath of crisp night air. "Are you ready to know?"

She nodded, her eyes glinting with anticipation. "Let's get this party started."

Riley and Lucy joined hands over the lighter, moving as one to touch the flickering flame to the special fireworks they'd ordered to celebrate the gender reveal.

Blue or pink?

As they stepped back, the fuse crackled and sparked, burning toward the boxed cannon of pyrotechnics. The explosion shot upward in a shriek of light, reaching higher and higher until fireworks lit the sky in a shower of silver, gold and…pink.

"It's a girl!" George announced to all, jumping

up and down so hard he punched holes in the snow. "Hooray! I'm gonna have a baby sister."

Congratulations ricocheted around them as Riley swooped Lucy up into a hug—his best friend, the love of his life. His breath hitched in his throat, his world brighter than the sparks exploding in the sky as he pictured that moment the four of them would become a family.

Riley smiled down at his wife. What an amazing word. Wife. "I sure do love you."

"Well, aren't we lucky?" She hooked her arms around his neck. "Because I love you too."

Pickles bounded over, running circles around them, corralling Riley and Lucy even closer together like a little matchmaker.

Not that anyone was resisting.

Riley kissed Lucy, or maybe she kissed him. He wasn't sure who'd moved first. He just reveled in the fireworks they shared as they welcomed the New Year and their new life together building the family of their dreams.

* * * * *

*For more cowboy Christmas romances,
try these other great stories:*

A Kiss at the Mistletoe Rodeo
By Kathy Douglass

His Baby No Matter What
By Melissa Senate

Sleigh Ride with the Rancher
By Stella Bagwell

*Available now wherever Harlequin
Special Edition books and ebooks are sold!*

WE HOPE YOU ENJOYED
THIS BOOK FROM

⊕ HARLEQUIN
SPECIAL
EDITION

Believe in love. Overcome obstacles. Find happiness.

Relate to finding comfort and strength in the
support of loved ones and enjoy the journey
no matter what life throws your way.

6 NEW BOOKS AVAILABLE EVERY MONTH!

HSEHALO2021

#2875 DREAMING OF A CHRISTMAS COWBOY
Montana Mavericks: The Real Cowboys of Bronco Heights
by Brenda Harlen

In the Christmas play she wrote and will soon star in, Susanna Henry gets the guy. In real life, however, all-grown-up Susanna is no closer to hooking up with rancher Dean Abernathy than she was at seventeen. Until a sudden snowstorm strands them together overnight in a deserted theater...

#2876 SLEIGH RIDE WITH THE RANCHER
Men of the West • by Stella Bagwell

Sophia Vandale can't deny her attraction to rancher Colt Crawford, but when it comes to men, trusting her own judgment has only led to heartbreak. Maybe with a little Christmas magic she'll learn to trust her heart instead?

#2877 MERRY CHRISTMAS, BABY
Lovestruck, Vermont • by Teri Wilson

Every day is Christmas for holiday movie producer Candy Cane. But when she becomes guardian of her infant cousin, she's determined to rediscover the real thing. When she ends up snowed in with the local grinch, however, it might take a Christmas miracle to make the season merry...

#2878 THEIR TEXAS CHRISTMAS GIFT
Lockharts Lost & Found • by Cathy Gillen Thacker

Widow Faith Lockhart Hewitt is getting the ultimate Christmas gift in adopting an infant boy. But when the baby's father, navy SEAL lieutenant Zach Callahan, shows up, a marriage of convenience gives Faith a son and a husband! But she's already lost one husband and her second is about to be deployed. Can raising their son show them love is the only thing that matters?

#2879 CHRISTMAS AT THE CHÂTEAU
Bainbridge House • by Rochelle Alers

Viola Williamson's lifelong dream to run her own kitchen becomes a reality when she accepts the responsibility of executive chef at her family's hotel and wedding venue. What she doesn't anticipate is her attraction to the reclusive caretaker whose lineage is inexorably linked with the property known as Bainbridge House.

#2880 MOONLIGHT, MENORAHS AND MISTLETOE
Holliday, Oregon • by Wendy Warren

As a new landlord, Dr. Gideon Bowen is more irritating than ingratiating. Eden Berman should probably consider moving. But in the spirit of the holidays, Eden offers her friendship instead. As their relationship ignites, it's clear that Gideon is more mensch than menace. With each night of Hanukkah burning brighter, can Eden light his way to love?

*In the Christmas play she wrote and will soon star
in, Susanna Henry gets the guy. In real life, however,
all-grown-up Susanna is no closer to hooking up with
hardworking rancher Dean Abernathy than she was
at seventeen. Until a sudden snowstorm strands them
together overnight in a deserted theater...*

*Read on for a sneak peek at
the final book in the Montana Mavericks:
The Real Cowboys of Bronco Heights continuity,*
Dreaming of a Christmas Cowboy,
by Brenda Harlen!

"You're cold," Dean realized, when Susanna drew her
knees up to her chest and wrapped her arms around her
legs, no doubt trying to conserve her own body heat as
she huddled under the blanket draped over her shoulders
like a cape.

"A little," she admitted.

"Come here," he said, patting the space on the floor
beside him.

She hesitated for about half a second before scooting
over, obviously accepting that sharing body heat was the
logical thing to do.

But as she snuggled against him, her head against
his shoulder, her curvy body aligned with his, there was
suddenly more heat coursing through his veins than Dean

had anticipated. And maybe it was the normal reaction for a man in close proximity to an attractive woman, but this was *Susanna*.

He wasn't supposed to be thinking of Susanna as an attractive woman—or a woman at all.

She was a friend.

Almost like a sister.

But she's not your sister, a voice in the back of his head reminded him. *So there's absolutely no reason you can't kiss her.*

Don't do it, the rational side of his brain pleaded. *Kissing Susanna will change everything.*

Change is good. Necessary, even.

When Susanna tipped her head back to look at him, obviously waiting for a response to something she'd said, all he could think about was the fact that her lips were *right there*. That barely a few scant inches separated his mouth from hers.

He only needed to dip his head and he could taste those sweetly curved lips that had tempted him for so long, despite all of his best efforts to pretend it wasn't true.

Not that he had any intention of breaching that distance.

Of course not.

Because this was *Susanna*.

No way would he ever—

Apparently the signals from his brain didn't make it to his mouth, because it was already brushing over hers.

Don't miss
Dreaming of a Christmas Cowboy *by Brenda Harlen,*
available December 2021 wherever
Harlequin Special Edition books and ebooks are sold.

Harlequin.com

SPECIAL EXCERPT FROM

HQN

*Angi Guilardi needs a man for Christmas—at least,
according to her mother. Balancing work and her
eight-year-old son, she has no time for romance…until
Angi runs into Gabriel Carlyle. Temporarily helping at
his grandmother's flower shop, Gabriel doesn't plan
to stick around, especially after he bumps into Angi,
one of his childhood bullies. But with their undeniable
chemistry, they're both finding it hard to stay away from
each other…*

Read on for a sneak preview of
Mistletoe Season,
the next book in USA TODAY *bestselling author
Michelle Major's Carolina Girls series,
available October 2021!*

"Who's dating?" Josie, who sat in the front row, leaned
forward in her chair.

"No one," Gabe said through clenched teeth.

"Not even a little." Angi offered a patently fake smile.
"I'd be thrilled to work with Gabe. I'm sure he'll have
lots to offer as far as making this Christmas season in
Magnolia the most festive ever."

The words seemed benign enough on the surface, but
Gabe knew a challenge when he heard one.

"I have loads of time to devote to this town," he said solemnly, placing a hand over his chest. He glanced down at Josie and her cronies and gave his most winsome smile. "I know it will make my grandma happy."

As expected, the women clucked and cooed over his devotion. Angi looked like she wanted to reach around Malcolm and scratch out Gabe's eyes, and it was strangely satisfying to get under her skin.

"Well, then." Mal grabbed each of their hands and held them above his head like some kind of referee calling a heavyweight boxing match. "We have our new Christmas on the Coast power couple."

Don't miss
Mistletoe Season *by Michelle Major,*
available October 2021 wherever HQN books
and ebooks are sold.

HQNBooks.com